THE BALLAD of DINGUS MAGEE

David Markson

COUNTERPOINT

BERKELEY

For Johanna and Jed

Library of Congress Cataloging-in-Publication Data
Markson, David.
The ballad of Dingus Magee / David Markson.
p. cm.
ISBN-13: 978-1-58243-410-0
ISBN-10: 1-58243-410-7
1. Outlaws—Fiction. I. Title.
PS3563.A67B35 2008
813'.54—dc22
2007043828

Cover design by Anita van de Ven
Interior design by David Bullen Design
Printed in the United States of America

Counterpoint
2117 Fourth Street
Suite D
Berkeley, CA 94710

www.counterpointpress.com
Distributed by Publishers Group West

10   9   8   7   6   5   4   3   2   1

THE BALLAD OF DINGUS MAGEE

Being the Immortal True Saga of
the Most Notorious and Desperate
Bad Man of the Olden Days,
his Blood-Shedding,
his Ruination of Poor Helpless Females,
& Cetera;
also including the Only Reliable Account
ever offered to the Public
of his Heroic Gun Battle
with Sheriff C. L. Hoke Birdsill,
Yerkey's Hole, New Mex., 1884,
and with Additional Commentary on
the Fateful and Mysterious
Bordello-Burning of the Same Year;
and
furthermore interspersed with
Trustworthy and Shamelessly Interesting
Sketches of "Big Blouse" Belle Nops,
Anna Hot Water, "Horseface" Agnes,
and Others,
hardly any Remaining Upright
at the End.
Composed in the Finest Modern English
as taken diligently from
the Genuine Archives by

DAVID MARKSON

"This is funny."

Doc Holliday, Dying Words

1

---

*"Pull off my boots.
I promised my mother
I'd never die with my boots on."*

Billy Clanton, The O.K. Corral, Tombstone, 1881

Turkey Doolan's crotch itched. His scalp was gamy. Poised in the saddle, with one freckled hand inside his jeans and several stumpy fingers of the other beneath his sombrero, he relieved himself by scratching simultaneously and with vehemence.

But Turkey's complaint was also mental. He knew this for a true fact as he shifted his buttocks athwart the hot leather, waiting while his companion emerged from a sheltered turning on the trail behind him. "Because I done rode with him for almost two weeks now," he reasoned, "and still there ain't nothing happened. Even accompanied with Mister Dingus Billy Magee hisself, and it ain't happened yet."

Up ahead, where the trail shelved gradually onto a low broad mesa, Turkey had noticed a cavalry patrol approaching in the distance. "But it ain't about to happen in the middle of no sweaty desert neither," he knew.

What he was waiting for made something of a story. He was the only child of an itinerant tinker who died when he, Turkey, was nine, and it might have had its beginnings even before that. Because he seemed ready even then, looking ahead solemnly to the occurrence of some fabulous and

unpredicated event of which only he, privately, had any intimation. He waited three years in the fourth grade alone.

They risked him behind a counter then (he had a stepfather now, a feed merchant), but there was small point in it.
The boy couldn't calculate, or wouldn't, and weights and
measures eluded him like ritual gossip mouthed in Pawnee.
"At least if you'd make an error once in *my* favor," the stepfather said. The first time they found no alternative to trusting him alone for an afternoon, this on a day in July of 1876,
Turkey loaded several hundred-pound sacks of meal onto
a stranger's wagon and accepted payment in Confederate
currency.

They tried in the local smithy next. He was indoctrinated
by a recalcitrant mule the first morning, profoundly enough
to be unable to sit for a week. Yet after that he seemed to get
on, and it even looked that he had a way with horses. "I'm
right glad to hear of it," the stepfather told the blacksmith,
"even if he had to be next month to thirteen before I found
out." "Found out what?" the blacksmith asked. "That the
one lesson he'll take to is the kind gets drove home with the
hind legs of a jackass," the stepfather said.

He held the job for more than two years, although he was
still waiting. It was part of him wholly now; he confronted
mule and man alike with the same vapidly anticipatory dim
gaze. "One day," he would tell himself. "Sure as shootin', one
day it's gonter happen."

Yet he could have remained at the smith's forever if it had
not been for the girl, the farmer's daughter. They were in the
loft when the farmer chanced in, and even then it might have
been all right, had the girl not inadvertently dropped her
frock over the side a moment before. The farmer gazed at the
garment for perhaps four seconds where it had draped itself
across a buckboard wheel, which was long enough for Turkey to deposit a saddle on his head. The man was on his feet
again immediately. "But doubtless it weren't gonter occur
around that dull old town anyways," Turkey had already
convinced himself.

It was scarcely about to happen on the trail either. Home

had been Missouri, and Turkey's last silver was gone before he crossed the Panhandle. He signed on herding sheep.

That was his first mistake. Not asking why there appeared to be no other hired hands on the ranch was the second. He had been in the pasture less than two hours when a torrent of longhorn steers came bellowing out from beneath a canopy of dust to wreak predictable enough havoc upon sheep and pasture both, if not to say almost upon Turkey himself. But if he galloped clear of the steers he did not escape the horsemen driving them. "This here's cattle territory, Cousin," they let him know. A fractured jaw and a sprung rib reiterated the declaration.

Half a day later, on a back road to nowhere except away, three nondescript men in a flat-bottom wagon pulled up beside him. This was when he began to get the idea that if and when it ever did come to pass, whatever it was, he wasn't going to have much luck with it. "Sheep or cattle, Brother?" one of the riders asked. Turkey had an ache in his face, another in his kidney. "Sure, boys," he said. "Cattle, boys, all down the line." No one had told him how protractile the war was, or how various its minions. When he hit the roadbed the sheepmen took turns walking on him.

Some hours later he ventured toward a farmhouse to ask a meal. He was shown eight inches of open slat in a Comanche shooting blind and the muzzle of a twelve-gauge shotgun. "State your allegiance, Uncle," a female voice demanded.

"Aw, lady," Turkey pleaded, already backing off, "you say first, huh?"

This set the tone. Once in a while he worked at a forge again, which seemed safe enough, but the jobs would never last. They couldn't, because he was still waiting. So when he took to theft it wasn't out of greed, or any motive other than the prosaic demands of necessity, of survival. He never became fully adept, never professional. Chickens were his strong suit, sometimes calves young enough to be lashed across a pommel. Perhaps once a year in some isolated back-trail town he would discover a cashbox that was not being watched too closely, or by anyone too acute.

But still it failed to happen, and after four long, unregenerate years he began to sense a certain disillusionment, even something of annoyance. One day he found himself deep in the New Mexico territory without even chickory for his coffee. "All right, then," he said. "So I reckon it's about time I made it happen on my own."

So when he chanced upon his next wayside cantina he paid no attention at all to the handsome, well-combed gelding tethered without. The cantina's door was open, and when he stepped into the gloom a rusted, secondhand 1873 Colt Peacemaker was at the operative position in his fist. "All right, boys," he growled, "let's do the business, everybody's hands up and I'll take whatever you're holding, cash money and don't omit the watches neither!"

There were two people in the cool windowless dusk. The pigtailed Chinaman behind the bar gazed at him incredulously, without other response. The young man reclining with his boots on the lone table and with a tankard of beer in his hand did not raise the beer, nor did he lower his boots. "Durn it, now," Turkey grunted, "dint you hear me, boys? I'm riled and I'm luckless, and that can make a man mighty mean."

"Sure can," the young man with the beer said.

"You're jest asking me for trouble, boys," Turkey said.

"Who says, now?"

Turkey finally got around to considering him. He was probably Turkey's own age, which was nineteen. He was slight, and his boots against the tabletop evidenced their newness and their cost. He wore a fringed red-and-yellow Mexican wool vest. And he smiled and smiled, from under fair unruly hair and a memorable sombrero.

But Turkey was looking at the weapons now also. The youth bore a gleaming sheathed revolver on each hip, slung low and almost plumbing the floor where his chair was tilted backward, and a third revolver lay between his heels on the table, evidently removed there from his waistband. Behind his chair a repeating Winchester rifle slanted against the peeling adobe. Next to that a shotgun reposed.

And something was happening to Turkey now at that, at last it truly was. "You got aholt of yourself yet?" the seated youth asked.

"Aw, now," Turkey said.

"Have a *cerveza*," the youth said.

Turkey had begun to scratch himself. "I seen your pitcher," he pronounced, "drawed on a 'Wanted' poster. You're Mister Dingus Billy Magee."

"Have a *cerveza*, seeing as how you got holt of yourself."

"Aw, now," Turkey said. "Aw, now, I dint mean nothing."

"Ain't nobody said otherwise."

Turkey shuffled toward the table, tickled pink. Already he could hear himself talking about it. "Boys, yes sir, one day over there to the New Mex, I had me a drink with Mister Dingus Billy Magee hisself."

He finally got close enough, still scratching, when Mister Dingus Billy Magee, desperado whom Turkey had long since cherished as a paradigm, reached up and clobbered him back of the ear with a fourth revolver that had been concealed below the chair in his other hand.

So the sense of expectation was greater than ever now. Because that was almost two weeks ago, and a man could not ride with Dingus Billy Magee for two weeks without something extraordinary coming to pass; Turkey surmised this for a fact. Dingus had magnanimously dismissed the circumstances of their meeting, this after Turkey had awakened beneath the table the following morning, and a few days later had even made Turkey a gift of the gaudy red-and-yellow Mexican vest. Turkey had discovered several bullet holes in the garment.

"I shouldn't oughter accept it, Dingus," he protested. "Duds a feller's been shot at in, it's sort of sentimental."

But if he rode with pride and assurance now, it was also with a certain bafflement. Because they had been moving undeviatingly across the flat, hot, seemingly endless mesa since that first morning, yet with neither aim nor object that Turkey could perceive. They were headed generally west; he fathomed that much without difficulty, because the mountains of Old Mexico remained always at their left. But not once had Dingus offered a word about what was in his mind.

So Turkey kept on waiting. That was what he was doing now, after the two weeks, scratching his groin on an otherwise unstimulating sultry afternoon as Dingus moved up from behind him to contemplate the cavalry patrol approaching slowly along the ragged trail. There were some dozen troopers, led by a captain whose braid they could discern from a considerable remove. Dingus greeted the sight with contempt. "Bunch of Fettermans," he snorted.

"What's a fetterman?" Turkey wanted to know.

"You never heard of Fetterman?"

"Don't reckon."

Dingus grimaced. "Fetterman was this brave captain they had somewheres—up to Fort Phil Kearny—used to brag he could take eighty men and ride smack through the whole Sioux nation. So comes one time they have to rescue this wagon train, and off goes Fetterman with jest the eighty men he always bragged on. *Ptheww! Ptheww!* Sioux and Cheyenne and Arapahoes under every bush. And this brave Fettermen, not only is he mortally shot hisself, but all the rest of them soljers get mortally shot likewise. The complete eighty."

"They wasn't all killed, was they?"

But the troopers were almost abreast of them now, pacing their mounts at a walk. It became evident that they had been in the field for some time, since both horses and men were grime-streaked and dusty.

"You think it's okay if'n they see you?" Turkey thought abruptly to whisper. "I mean, suppose they read some posters like I done?"

"Who, them Fettermans? They're too busy keeping their heads down, smelling out Apache ponyshit along the trails."

"Apaches? I ain't heard tell of Apaches lately a-tall."

" 'Course not. They're all down to Old Mex, pausing for

springtime papoose-producing. That's what makes these Fettermans so brave."

The troopers were wearily passing them then, not halting, however, with the exception of the captain, who reined to one side. He was quite young, and mud had caked at the yellow stripe of his right thigh. His name, *Fiedler,* was etched into his tooled saddle.

"Morning, Captain Fetterman, sir," Dingus said affably.

The captain spun toward them.

Dingus was innocent. "Handsome-looking troop. I said you can't get any *better men,* indeed. Reminds me, my chum and me, here, we cut some Apache sign this morning."

Lifting his unshaven jaw, the captain scowled. "Mescalero? Near here?"

"Them or Chiricahuas. Right shameful, the way that Geronimo's still running loose. Burning folks' homes, looting and pillaging. Why, them two wagons never had a chance."

"Wagons?" The captain was open-eyed now. "What wagons? You saw two wagons that—"

" 'Bout six hours' lazy walk, the way we jest come." Dingus gestured gravely. "My chum and me, we buried the men, poor devils, it appeared the Christian thing to do. But there was lady's clothing all scattered, so I reckon old Gee'mo done appropriated the womenfolk. Must be all raped bow-legged by now. You can pick up the trail, most like, if you—"

But the captain, ashen, had already spurred his mount. He shouted a command and the troopers fell into a gallop, skittering off.

—And that was Dingus Billy Magee. "Oh, you're a belly-busting caution, you are," Turkey told him as they stepped out. He rode now grinning from ear to ear.

But Dingus fell behind him almost at once, as was his curious habit. He rode huddled low in the saddle also, another characteristic, sitting slope-shouldered as if resigned to an incessant rain. "Tell me somethin'," Turkey asked idly after a period. "There any special reason, we jest keep roaming on west like we been?"

For a time Dingus did not answer, coming ahead in that hunched way, and Turkey himself was still preoccupied enough with the recent prank so that another minute passed before he finally became sensible of the other's expression. And then it was too late. "You ever wondered what kind of a commotion it would make," Dingus was asking, "if'n a feller went and stuck a gun into each of your ears, and then squeezed off both triggers at the same time? What do you reckon them shots would sound like from inside your head?"

And this too, this abruptly, was Dingus. Hardly amused now, Turkey flopped limply about in the saddle. "Aw, now why do you want to go talking about a thing like that?"

"You reckon you'd hear two sounds, maybe? One when you was shot, and again when them two bullets met head-on inside there?"

"Aw, Dingus—"

"A feller don't like persons to go questioning his private intentions," Dingus said.

"Aw, Dingus—"

"Git on along," Dingus said.

Turkey sighed as he shifted forward again, heeling up a slight incline. He rode sullenly.

So when Dingus decided to speak once more, an hour or so later, it was only to disconcert him further. "Turkey," he asked, "now where in the copulating damn did you come by that there chapeau?"

Turkey eyed him tentatively.

"I wouldn't give away a hat like that to a pee-drinking Injun. Shames a man to be seed riding with you. Here now, you take mine—"

Confused and overcome at once, Turkey commenced to scratch himself. "But that there's your 'spensive sombrero—"

"Gonter grab me up a new one right soon anyways."

"Right soon—?"

But again Dingus did not elaborate. Content once more nonetheless, Turkey pridefully inspected the bullet hole in the sombrero's brim, failing to realize that the trail had forked into an actual wagon road that Dingus was indicating they should follow. Then, startled, Turkey pulled up short.

"Say, this here direction—ain't this the direction on into Yerkey's Hole?"

"Looks that way."

"And ain't Yerkey's Hole the town where Mister Hoke Birdsill is sheriff?"

"Last I heard," Dingus agreed.

So Turkey paused to consider that. And then he commenced to get it again, that old indomitable feeling.

"You fretted over something?" Dingus wanted to know.

"Jest over that Hoke Birdsill, is all. I reckon he sure makes it *his* business to know your face, even if them soljers never done—especially since he were forced to study on it every day when you was his prisoner that once, until you escaped on him and he vowed he'd git you."

"Aw, that's only old Hoke."

"That mean it's true what they say?"

"Depends what they say, most like."

"That you and Hoke Birdsill was supposed to be real tender poontang-sharing chums but then he turned to being a lawman and you turned to being a desperado and so he's gonter gun you down because it don't look right, a lawman having a feller like Dingus Billy Magee for a old poontang-sharing chum—that true?"

"Hoke still says that, that him and me was fond chums?"

"What I hear," Turkey said.

"Me and Hoke Birdsill," Dingus considered. "Well now, you mean to say I dint never tell you how it come about that Hoke got to telling folks what dear chums we was?"

Turkey said nothing, but he had brought his horse almost to a standstill. For a moment Dingus gazed off into space, privately amused. "Old Hoke," he said then. "Oh, I knowed him a little, here and yon, I reckon, but never no more than saying howdy, you understand? And then some time goes by, and there was a couple of them piddling rewards on me by then—back a spell, hardly nothing much more than several thousand dollars all told, maybe—and Hoke had got hisself a badge by then likewise. So one day I'm on the prod over this way, and I break a cinch on my saddle. Weren't nothing, but while I'm getting her fixed I hear this other horse, and when I look up, darned if'n it ain't old Hoke. Well, now. So he sits there a time, and I stand there a time, and then he says, 'Howdy, Dingus,' and so I say, 'Howdy, Hoke.' And then he says, 'I got to arrest you, I reckon.' Well, that were *his* poor misunderstanding, you see, only he dint know that yet, because there was the small matter of I'd *heard* him before he'd seed me—so what am I holding onto behind my horse but this here difficulty-equalizing old shotgun." Dingus stroked the weapon as they moved, chuckling. "Well, old Hoke. He gets around to where he notices that, finally, and he turns the color of a shoat's belly, I reckon. 'Now, Hoke,' I say then, 'you wasn't truly gonter arrest me, was you?' 'Now, Dingus,' Hoke says. 'You was jest tasting that there reward money, wasn't you, Hoke?' I ask him; 'you was right hungry for it, wasn't you?' 'Now, Dingus,' Hoke says. Then round about that time I notice that jest under where Hoke is sitting his horse, there's a mule or a burro been there first, you see, and it's left a reminder. All heaped up higher'n a small boy's first arising, and right fresh too. So I inform old Hoke, 'Hoke, I'll tell you what. You being so hungry, you climb on down and eat, then.' Well, poor Hoke. A man'd do pretty near any-thing in this old world to stop a shotgun from going off in the very nearby vicinity of his stomach, I reckon. But wouldn't you know—right about then, darned if'n that weren't when the loopy-nozzled critter took to informing folks how good he knowed me. Yep. 'Do I know Dingus Billy Magee?' old Hoke would say, '—why jest a short spell back, Dingus and me, we ate chow together—'"

That might have been four o'clock. Roughly two hours later, into dusk, Turkey found out what he had been waiting for. For most of the two hours he had been concentrating on it deliciously, the anticipation gripping him like a mustard plaster. And then when it happened it was typical that for a moment he was thinking about something else altogether.

They had just turned aside from the road itself, to follow a little-used trail behind the town's first dilapidated outlying miners' shacks, when this other thing occurred to him. It stiffened him in the saddle. "Yerkey's Hole!" he cried. "I plumb forgot."

Dingus came huddling along hatless after him. "What's that?" he asked. "Them prosty-toots. They still got all them prosty-toots here?"

"Old Turkey. Now jest what else outside of ripe titty do you reckon would make a feller ride full across the New Mex territory?"

"Huh?"

"Git along, Turkey."

"Well, hang me for a horse-stealer." Turkey almost kicked his mount into a gallop at the wonderment of it.

So then they shot him.

He was just passing the rear of a livery, the first imposing building in the town, and the light thrown by the single lamp near the back entrance seemed scarcely enough. So when he heard the shout, with whores still uppermost in his mind, he never thought to spur clear. "Great gawd, it's him!" it seemed the voice said, and then a horse was clomping hard by Turkey's ear, and then something else was being yelled that he never did comprehend. There were five or six shots, at the least.

So he had time; he might well have told himself "Turkey, it sure is happening now, it absolutely and truly is happening at that." Instead he floated there in the saddle, actually with one hand poised to commence scratching, in fact, until something that felt like a thrown anvil nudged him in the ribs, and after that something else he was fairly certain was ground collided with his head, and so all he told himself was, "Well, if that ain't my luck, sure enough."

For a long while then everything was remarkably peaceful, and remarkably quiet too, except for the soft measured sound of dripping that Turkey was positive came from inside of him somewhere, although he was far too weary to sit up and solve it.

"Did you git 'im, Hoke?" a faraway voice said at last.

"What do you reckon that is alaying out there, you addle-brained fool?"

"Is he dead?"

"How the thunderation should I know?"

"Ain't you going out to see?"

"And take a chance I get my brains blowed out?"

The voices stopped then, or faded beyond hearing, so Turkey began to talk instead. "It looks like I'm kilt, boys," he said, although not loudly. "Put it down that I were riding with Dingus Billy Magee, will you do me that little thing, boys?"

But nobody did him any little thing. Turkey could see an incarnadine sky, and the glow from the stable off to one side, but nearby nothing moved. Then the voices came again.

"You aiming to jest leave him lay there, Hoke?"

"You go, you're so all-fired anxious."

"Ain't said one word about being anxious. Jest a mite curious, is all."

"Well, shut your yap then and leave me do it my way."

"Don't look like much of a way, jest ducked down here back of a cow."

So it might have been ten minutes, perhaps only five. Turkey continued to hear the dripping, which eventually slowed. Finally he was able to perceive shadows looming nearby.

"Keep me covered good, now—"

"I got dead bead on his skull, Hoke—"

"Well, keep it that way."

The shadows came closer, with infinite slowness. Then, hovering near him, one of them paused. It hung there for a time, disembodied.

"Dead, Hoke?"

"Oh, that miserable varmint! Oh, that double-dealing, nooky-snatching, sneaky-assed skunk! I'll—I'll—"

"What's that, Hoke?"

"I'll crucify him! I swear, this time I'll murder the little sidewinder if'n it's the ultimate mortal deed I do on this earth! I'll bend his mangy dong in half and stomp on it like—"

"How's that again?"

"Ain't him. Ain't Dingus."

"That's Dingus's red-and-yeller vest there, ain't it?"

Turkey Doolan smiled. "He give me the hat too, boys," he proclaimed. "We was right fond chums, me and Dingus William Magee."

"Sure, it's Dingus's vest," the voice said, ignoring him. "And that makes three blasted times in six months I done put a bullet clean through the turd-wiping thing, too—with some other hero-worshiping durned imbecile wearing it every blasted time!"

But Turkey Doolan had stopped attending. He listened to the dripping instead. There was little question, it had happened. Turkey was at ease.

2

---

*"No, by heaven! I never
killed a man without good cause."*

Wild Bill Hickok, quoted by Henry M. Stanley

As a normal thing, Sheriff C. L. Hoke Birdsill affected a cut-away frock coat, striped pants, and a vest with a chain from which the tiny gold star of his office was sported. He also wore a derby, usually brown.

It had not always been so. Indeed, Hoke was thirty-one, and if he allowed himself the vanity of such sartorial excesses it was because until less than one year before he had never owned much more than the shirt on his back, which smelled generally of cow. Nor had he been a sheriff then either.

But then one day he had awakened with a pain in his chest. He tried to ignore it, but when it persisted, and severely enough to keep him out of the saddle, meaning out of work as a trail hand, he visited a doctor in Santa Fe. The doctor diagnosed consumption and gave Hoke twelve months to live.

This staggered him, less because he did not particularly care to die than because he had no notion how to cope with his time until then (he had never been especially burdened with imagination). He drifted to Fort Worth, for no particular reason. He had very little cash, but he took to gambling anyway. So then an incredible run of luck was to dumfound him all the more. Within short weeks he had won eleven hundred dollars, more money than he had ever seen at one time in his life and certainly far more than he would need to get through the remaining days of it.

Perhaps he was conscious of the irony. In any case he decided he might as well live according to his new means, which was when he began buying the clothes. "At least I'll be buried in style," he told himself. He was a tall man with a long, leaden face who had always been rail-thin but now believed himself cadaverous, and he grew a mustache also, which came out orange (his hair was quite dark, almost black). He had sold his horse and saddle and virtually all the rest of his gear, save for a single Smith and Wesson .44-caliber revolver in its sheath that he infrequently wore. He took to strolling considerable distances about the town or sitting wordlessly on his hotel's porch. Probably he looked thoughtful. Possibly he was. He wrote the projected date beneath his signature when he made arrangements with a bewildered local mortician and paid the man full cash in advance.

Then one morning he sat bolt upright in his bed some hours before dawn, startled by a realization that should have come to him weeks earlier, even before he had arrived in Forth Worth. His room was chilly, but when he undid his long woolen underwear, clutching at his chest, he found he was sweating. By the time he reached the stairway beyond his door, wholly without regard for sartorial propriety now, he was running, sprinting down through the darkened lobby and into the street. The nearest signboard he could recall was two blocks away, on a quiet side road, and he achieved it in no more than a minute. It was a woman who finally opened, and had she not been the wife of a doctor for forty years she might reasonably have taken Hoke Birdsill for mad. "Yes," she said, "all right, he's dressing, he won't be a moment, perhaps if you would tell me what it is—"

But he had already sprung past her. The doctor was in his woolens, climbing into his trousers. "I ain't got it," Hoke said, or rather sobbed. Only the sight of a second turned-down bed, the woman's, gave him pause. But if he hesitated long enough to catch his breath he made no move to back out again. "It's a month and I ain't," he gasped. "I got so used to thinking about dying from it that I reckon I forgot all about having to live with it first, because—"

The doctor had paused with one leg raised, gawking. "What? Live with—?"

"Not for a month. More than that. I can't remember when I had it last. Not when I sold my horse or won all that there money or went to the undertaker's or—"

"What? Listen now, I still don't . . . do you mean to say you've come barging in here at four o'clock in the morning to tell me about some pain you haven't got, haven't had since . . . what undertaker? Listen, are you all right? Do you feel—?"

The doctor had to throw him out, at the point of a Sharps Buffalo gun. Hoke did not notice until it finally materialized under his chin. So he waited until six o'clock for the next one, and then he saw three doctors in half as many hours. They all told him the same thing. If they weren't positive about what it had been in Santa Fe (two suggested indigestion, one ventured gas) they were unanimous about what it wasn't now. Hoke jumped a stage before noon.

He returned to Santa Fe first. He found the original doctor, in the same office. "That's a shame," he told the man, "you ought to have been gone." The man did not recognize him. "Birdsill," Hoke said. "C. L. Hoke Birdsill. I'm gonter die in ten months from the consumption." "Oh, yes, of course," the doctor said, "I remember now. Well, and how are you feeling, Mr. Birdsoak?" "Fine," Hoke said, "and how do you feel, Doc?" "I?" the doctor said, "oh, I'm fine, fine, never sick a day in my life." "You know the date?" Hoke asked him, "today's date?" The doctor glanced at a calendar and read it off. "Remember it," Hoke said. The doctor was an unassertive soul, an Easterner, and he began to tremble the moment Hoke took hold of his shirtfront. "Keep it in mind good," Hoke said, "because on this same day next year, one full year from today, I'm gonter come back here and shoot you square between the ears." "But you'll be dead by then yourself," the doctor protested. "Then you'll be jest lucky," Hoke told him.

Yet the truth of the matter was that Hoke actually owed the man a debt of gratitude, a fact which dawned on him about now. He was through punching cattle, nor was it simply a matter of the clothes. During his stay in Texas he had also discovered he liked the feel of a bed.

The next coach he took was posted for California. He picked California mainly because he had no idea what was to come next in his resurrected life, and that appeared as good a place to muse on it as any. One notion that had crossed his mind was that he might open a saloon. Another was that he might serve as a peace officer somewhere, though he had no idea how one went about this last. He had some eight hundred dollars left.

But he was not to achieve the coast, and only in part because old habit had made him too frugal to pay for more than piecemeal passage. It was at a meal stop some hours shy of a place called Yerkey's Hole, which marked the limit of his current ticket, that nemesis entered Hoke Birdsill's life to alter it for eternity.

Hoke was the only passenger on the run, and he was eating without haste since the horses were likewise to be fed. So he was still at the table when the gelding cantered up outside the cantina and the youth dismounted. Hoke recognized the fringed red-and-yellow Mexican vest at once. "Why, howdy there, Dingus," he called.

"Well, will you look at Hoke Birdsill in the dude's duds. You come into some riches now, did you?"

"A middling piece of luck," Hoke allowed as the boy joined him. Hoke knew him only slightly, from random saloons. He thought him a pleasant lad. "Jest passing by, are you?"

Dingus gestured vaguely with a hand that Hoke now saw to be bandaged, or rather it was the wrist. "Thought I'd mosey over west fer some sporting life, maybe. Like as not try some stealing here and there too, I reckon."

"I heard tell you'd gone bad," Hoke said. "What do you want to perpetrate things that ain't lawful for, now?"

Dingus removed his sombrero, fanning air across his merry face. "Hot, ain't she?" he said. "Tell you the truth, Hoke, I don't rightly approve on it much neither, but a feller's got to live, and that's the all of it." He indicated the damaged wrist. "Sort of trying, too, what with lawmen taking pot shots at you like they do."

"Honest Injun?" Hoke's own forty-four had never served to enter contest with more than an occasional rattlesnake.

"Weren't nothing, really," Dingus said.

But abruptly Hoke grew uncomfortable. "That sure is a handsome-looking derby hat," the lad was adding. "Always did want to git me one of those, and that's a fact. Let's try her, eh Hoke?"

"I reckon not," Hoke said hastily. "I shed dandruff pretty bad."

"Let me jest inspect how she's manufactured then. I won't put her on."

"I reckon not," Hoke said again.

"Well, now. And I always pegged you fer a accomodating sort of feller, too."

"A man's clothes is his castle, is all," Hoke said, abandoning his meal. He called the proprietor. Deliberately, he withdrew a billfold in which he carried some seven paper dollars, allowing Dingus full scrutiny as he settled his accounting.

"Don't look like much remaining of that there luck," Dingus speculated.

Still distressed, Hoke said, "I were ill a spell in Fort Worth. I had to go to four doctors in one morning, it got so bad." He arose all too casually and strolled toward the stage.

"Ain't gonter climb back aboard without a pee, are you?" Dingus inquired, idly walking with him. "Gets right shaggy in a feller's crotch, he sweats in a dusty coach all morning. Nice to air her out, like, even if she's only got a little trickling to do."

"I reckon you got a point," Hoke admitted. They accompanied each other to a rear wall, reaching to unbutton in tandem.

"Jest keep a good strong holt there, Hoke," Dingus suggested then.

"Huh—?"

But it was far too late. Jerking his head just enough to see a revolver in the hand he had trusted to be otherwise occupied, Hoke urinated on his boot.

"I'll jest take a loan of that there derby hat, I reckon," Dingus decided. "A desperado's a desperado, but I kin leave a man his final few dollars, seeing as how you was sick."

Terrified by the looming weapon, though heartsick over far more than Dingus knew, Hoke closed his eyes as the outlaw reached to the derby. He sobbed miserably as his eight hundred dollars fluttered from within it to the ground.

"Well, howdy do!"

"Aw now, Dingus. Aw now, Dingus—"

Dingus was already squatting. "Back off there a step like a good feller, will you, Hoke?" he requested. "You're dribbling on some of my new twenties—"

So when he found himself stranded in Yerkey's Hole there was no saloon to be opened—nor would there be a bed either, or not for long. But there was still the job of sheriff to think about, urgently now and with certain expectations as it developed also, since the local man had only then struck it rich in the nearby mines and headed back east. Hoke sought out the town mayor.

"Who're you?" the mayor said. "C. L. Hoke Birdsill," Hoke told him. "Never heard of you," the mayor said. "Is that important?" Hoke wanted to know. "Of course it's important," the mayor said. "What we do, we pick some outlaw with a real foul reputation for meanness, usually some killer's been drove out of some other town and decides to raise a ruckus here. Safest that way. How do you think they picked that Wyatt Earp, over to Tombstone?" "Oh," Hoke said, "well, no harm in asking." "No harm 'tall," the mayor said. "Go get yourself a reputation, like say that feller Dingus Billy Magee, you mosey on back and we'll make you sheriff in jig time. Right smart derby hat you got on there—"

And then it was the derby that saved him. Or rather the local madam did, once she had seen the hat.

Her name was Belle Nops. Hoke had met her on occasion through the years, although as a cowhand he had never spoken more than a dozen words to the woman, and those strictly business. She intimidated him, as she did virtually everyone else. No one knew where she came from, although she had been something of a legend in the territory for a decade or more. She might have been forty, and she admitted to having been married once, if obscurely. She had arrived in Yerkey's Hole with one covered wagon and two girls, both Mexicans, and had set up business in a tent near the mines. Now the tent had long since become a house of exceptional size and intricate design (evidently it had been built originally to accommodate six girls, with new rooms added haphazardly and askew as the six became twelve and fifteen and twenty; finally there were even additional stories) replete with saloon, parlors, and piano. Some of the girls were white these days also.

Not that Hoke could afford any of either classification in his present circumstances. So he was both confused and complimented when she propositioned him. "A manager?" he said. "Me? And anyways, what kind of a job is—?"

She was a bawdy, overwhelming woman built like a dray horse and homely as sin, almost as tall as Hoke himself, if with an astonishing bosom nearly as famous as her house. Hoke had been in the bordello itself perhaps three times during his first week in town, and then only to nurse a solitary glass of cheap Mexican *pulque* in its saloon each time, nor was he conscious that she was even aware of his presence until she appeared at his table peremptorily and without preliminaries on the third of those nights to say, "You, Birdsill, down on your luck, ain't you? Come on—" She led him to a large room at the head of the main stairway which he expected to find an office and did, with a scarred desk in one corner and with a safe, but which was her bedroom also. Beneath a canopy of a sort Hoke had never seen except in pictures was a bed of a size he had not dreamed imaginable. He could not take his eyes from it. "What kind of manager?" he asked.

"Them duds," she told him. "Listen, if there's one thing on this earth a frazzle-peckered cowpoke or a dirty-bottomed miner respects, it's somebody he instinctively thinks is better than he is. You hang around in those fancy pants and you won't even have to tote a gun half the time."

"Gun?" Hoke said. "Oh. What you mean, you want somebody to hold the drunks in line?"

"And to count the take and keep the bartenders from robbing me blind and to bash the girls around too, maybe, when they get to feeling skittish. It's got too big; I can't watch it all by myself. All you'd have to do, you'd be here nights. I'll give you sixty a month, room and meals too, if you want that—"

"So I get to be a law officer, all right," Hoke thought, "excepting it's only in a whorehouse." Aloud he said, "What I'm supposed to be, it's a Colt-carrying pimp—"

"And what you mean is, you're afraid the boys will call you that. All right, we won't let anybody know you're working for me at all then. I'll make you sheriff of the whole ragged-assed town. Hell's bells, I own nine-tenths of the sleazy place anyway. The official sheriff's job pays forty—"

"But I thought a sheriff had to be—"

"What?"

"Never mind." Hoke was only half-listening anyway. He kept glancing toward that bed.

"That forty, and twenty more from me," Belle went on. "All right, it's only money—leave it at the original sixty from the house. That's a hundred altogether and you can live in the back room of the jail, and if you spend your nights here it'll look legitimate because we get all the action anyway—" She was standing. Hoke arose also, holding his derby. "So it's all set. I'll talk to the mayor tomorrow. We—"

"Lissen," Hoke said then. "That bed. Could I—?"

"Bed? Well naturally it's a bed. What else did you think it would be, a—"

"No. I meant some night. Or some afternoon when you're not here. Kin I jest try it out once, to see what it—"

"Some afternoon *what?* When I'm not where?" Belle Nops was scowling at him. "What are you talking about? Or rather what do you think *I'm* talking about? Come on now, and get shed of them duds. If they're too fancy to throw over a chair you can use the closet there. It's—"

"What?" Hoke said. "Use the—"

Belle Nops had already bent to disengage her skirts. "First man in the territory in half a year who looks like he's had a bath since the war ended. Well, come on, come on, you figure on doing it from where you're standing, maybe?"

"Oh," Hoke said. "Oh. No. I were jest—" He set down the derby. "So that's how a feller gets to be sheriff," he said, watching her emerge.

So if he had lost his eight hundred dollars he at least had the job he wanted now, not to mention use of that remarkable bed, among other unanticipated developments. The jail itself contained three cells and an office, and as it turned out he enjoyed this aspect of his work too. Days, he spent most of his time contemplating the warrants and the reward circulars that crossed his desk, including several for Dingus Billy Magee who it developed was worth some three thousand dollars, if not yet quite important enough to be wanted both dead and/or alive. At times Hoke apprehended an occasional drunk. "But don't let it get your johnny up," Belle Nops told him. "Anything that smells like it might start to involve gunshooting, you send a telegram to the federal marshal." "I aim to," Hoke said.

Probably he did, since he was satisfied with the arrangement precisely as it stood, and with Belle Nops herself for that matter, even if she did continue to intimidate him. Her attitude toward him was hardly less brusque, nor would

Hoke ever know when to expect a demand for his more personal services. Some nights he would find her staring at him
from across a room almost dubiously, or certainly with nothing like interest in her expression, let alone heat, but then a
nod, a gesture, even a ticlike curl of the mouth would indicate that he was wanted; or again he might feel a tap on his
shoulder at a poker or monte table and glance up to see her
already marching off, not looking back as she informed him
curtly, "Business matter in the office, Sheriff." Their actual
conjunction would be equally grim also, still with no more
than a nod of greeting at his appearance, although this would
change at once; Hoke would begin to hear immediately the
slow inexorable steady mouthing of the curses, the mounting vituperation and blasphemy which startled even him,
ex-cowhand, in tones flat and vicious yet somehow finally
perversely impassioned too, finally lost among the enormous
calving sounds and the heaving breath, the culmination.
Then before he himself could recover or think to remember
what she had been calling him she would be dressed and
gone again, once more indifferent and contemptuous and
sour. It was a little like wrestling a bear, and to no decision.
Thereafter Hoke would shrug and usually remain in the bed
for a time before wandering off to wait bleakly for his next
unforseeable summons. At other times he would go three or
even four days without so much as a word or sign from her
at all, often with no indication as they passed one another
in the parlors or corridors that she even knew him by sight.
Hoke was also somewhat chagrined by the second door in
her room, which opened onto a narrow outside stairway at
the rear of the house, although he had never actually seen
anyone make use of it. "But it seems a feller ought to know
he's got it exclusive for a spell, especially since she don't
appear to admire it none," he told himself.

Yet at moments like these he could not truly have said if
it were jealousy he felt or whether he simply missed the bed
itself. So then one night he lost bed and Belle both.

Then again by virtue of the same fateful occurrence he

was to find himself no longer merely an anonymous territorial sheriff but a man of parts and of fame, and with a newspaper cutting to prove it that he would carry in his billfold for years:

Hanging of Desperado

Dingus Billy Magee, that notorious desperado who has been terrorizing folks throughout the New Mex. Territory, has been sentenced to hang, and good riddance say God-fearing people. As has been stated by reliable persons, said Magee was captured after a deadly gun battle in the Territory by a stalwart law officer, Mr. C. L. Hoke Birdbottom, and more power to the likes of him. It needed a brave man indeed to face up to that cowardly and murderous outlaw and Sheriff Birdbottom was just that man. He deserves his various reward money and then some.

It happened after Hoke had worn the star about eight weeks, on a quiet Wednesday (most of Belle's trade came on weekends). Belle herself was holding court in one of the smaller parlors, dealing faro for Texas cattlemen in what experience had already taught Hoke would be an all-night session. He had himself dealt out of his own game, climbed the stairs, stripped to his woolens, and curled self-indulgently among the luxurious silk sheets.

He had no idea how long he had been asleep when he sensed the sagging of the mattress as it took the extra weight, and then almost instantly the two impatient arms fetched him close.

Still drowsy, yet puzzled vaguely by the coarse, familiarly tacky garment his own groping hands now touched, he muttered, "Well say, now, what kind of night duds you took to wearing there, Belle?"

"Great gawd almighty!" said a voice that was decidedly not his employer's. Nor was it even a woman's. "Hoke Birdsill? Is that Hoke? Well, I'll be a mule-sniffing son of a—"

They got to their guns simultaneously, vaulting to opposite sides of the sprawling, improbable field.

"What the thunderation?"

"Why, howdy do, Hoke!"

Hoke ducked, trembling. He could see the gleam of the revolver facing him. He presumed Dingus could see his own equally well.

"Least you could do is wake a man up afore you crawl betwixt his blankets, durn it," Hoke protested.

"Tell the truth, I weren't rightly expecting *you* in there—"

"I oughter blast you where you're squatting—"

"Don't reckon you could hit much in this dark, not any better'n I would."

Hoke thought about that. "I'll stand up and back off if you will," he suggested.

"We could hold a truce until we git some trousers on, I reckon."

"That's near to what I had in mind."

"Except I don't know as I could rightly trust you, Hoke. You still bearing a grudge about that money from your derby hat, are you?"

"I reckon I got the privilege."

"Sure enough. But I reckon I ain't gonter put aside this here Colt to climb into my pants then, neither."

So they squatted some more. "We'll just sort of hold tight 'til daylight then," Hoke said.

"Or 'til Belle comes in and heaves us both out."

"I never took you for a beau of Belle's, Dingus."

"Ain't nothing. Older women always do sort of cotton to me, seems. It's that boyish face I got, maybe. I never figured you for one, neither."

"Well—" Hoke paused, the seed of a solution in his mind now. "Tell you the truth, Dingus, I ain't no beau at that. I were jest sort of borrowing the bed fer a spell, is the truth of it."

"How's that?"

"Jest sleeping a spell."

"Well say, now, you mean you ain't come into any cash money since I divested that there chapeau? You mean things has got so bad you have to take the loan of a bed in a house of ill repute that ain't in use?"

"Things is pretty bad, all right—"

They continued to squat. Still thinking hard, Hoke said, "Jobs is difficult to come by hereabouts, Dingus. You'd know that if'n you'd been around. But you ain't been around lately, have you?"

"Been over east."

"Well, jobs is mighty scarce. Matter of fact, things is so bad—well, it jest come to me I'd like to throw in with you, if'n you ever take partners now and then?"

"I donno, Hoke. Sort of delicate, deciding to trust a feller bears you a grudge."

"I could forget the grudge right soon, once we achieved us some cash money, I reckon."

Dingus exhaled pensively, considering things. Hoke was still thinking for all he was worth. "My hand's off'n my gun on the bed there, Dingus—"

Dingus raised himself cautiously. "Back off slow, Hoke—"

"I'm abackin', Dingus—"

He saw the other weapon drop finally to the bed. They stood eyeing each other.

"Shucks," Hoke said reassuringly, "I reckon you *had* to take my poke that time, once you was started robbing my hat."

"Weren't no way out'n it, jest by the ethics of the thing."

"Sure. But meantimes, well, what's the sense to keep up a grudge against a feller's been my chum, even if I only knowed you here and yon? But say, I got to get this here bed tidied up before I go, or Belle is apt to skin me. You want to give me some assistance?"

"Thisaway? Durned if'n I ever tidied up a bed in my life."

"Thataway's pretty near. Wait'll I come round and direct you. What you got to do, you lean over more, sort of not touching it at the same time, so's you can leave the pillers all fluffed."

"Feller never knows when he's gonter learn something new, I reckon. This correct?"

"That's right dandy there, Dingus," Hoke told him. "And now jest sort of stay bent over a spell while I collect me your guns peaceable like, seeing as how I got my own aimed right into your miserable skull. What you jest learned, you polecat, it ain't how to tidy up a bed, but jest what bed you should of rode clear of to start with. And you can consider yourself lucky we ain't outside nowheres neither, or you can bet a cash dollar I'd make you pee down your woolens there too, jest to get us all the more evened up—"

But Hoke had been in the wrong bed also, or at least at the wrong time, because Belle Nops fired him the next morning. "But he's jest that desperado," Hoke pleaded, "he ought to be in jail anyways." "I don't care if he's Jesse James's pet hound," Belle told him. "What kind of sheriff do you think you are, galavanting around the countryside arresting outlaws when you were supposed to be keeping an eye on my whores!" "Well, I weren't even actually galavanting," Hoke insisted, "we was jest—" "Look, I don't care if you tell me you found him in that bed of mine you spend so much time in, which as a matter of fact you likely did, since the horny little twerp has come sneaking in there and tried to assault my bloomers at least three times since he stole a key one night. Which is—" "What?" Hoke said, "you mean he ain't your—?" "You'll never know jest what you lost, brother," she said. "You can keep that badge if you want to; I don't give a belch in a hot wind about that. But any juicy hocks you grab around here now, you'll pay the going rate among the girls or else go dig yourself up a squaw somewheres." "But Belle," Hoke said.

Yet it was considerably less calamitous than he thought, since there remained that reward money to compensate for the lost sinecure. First, however, a circuit judge had to be gotten hold of, to try Dingus. (The legalities themselves were remarkably informal. The judge arrived on mule-back, wearing a Remington revolver on each hip and with a Blackstone under one arm and a Bible beneath the other, and he confronted Dingus through the bars of his cell. "You Dingus Bobby Magee?" he asked. "I reckon that's close," Dingus allowed. "You assassinate all them critters we got warrants swore out to?" the judge asked. "How many assas-sinations you got?" Dingus said. "Guilty as charged," the judge declaimed, "and I hereby sentence you to be strung up by the neck and left strung until you are dead, dead, dead." "And you kin go plumb to hell, hell, hell," Dingus said.) But then the judge signed the execution order, and a deposition indicating that the said Magee was indeed in the custody of Sheriff C. L. Hoke Birdbill, Yerkey's Hole, New Mex., and once the latter had been posted to Santa Fe Hoke received his three thousand dollars. He secured it in a locked strong-box beneath a cot in the smallest unused cell, the cell locked in turn.

And he began to find his conventional sheriffdom more gratifying then also, what with the abrupt fame that had accrued to it. A San Antonio newspaper, from which he would clip the most commendatory of the several accounts of the sentencing, reposed upon his desk throughout the weeks he awaited the hangman.

"You're gonter get it memorized," the condemned man remarked of Hoke's attention to the paper, though with his new affluence Hoke had taken to browsing through a St. Louis mail-order catalog with almost equal frequency. Amused, or anyway unperturbed, Dingus lay with his boots off and a sombrero shading his eyes, on the cot within his cell. This was a Thursday night, with the execution finally but two days off.

"They do word it right pretty," Hoke acknowledged.

"But all the reference to that there deadly gun battle," Dingus speculated from beneath the hat; "you reckon that got wrote up too, I mean previous to this recenter story about the hanging?"

"I reckon," Hoke said, not pursuing it.

"I sure wish we could get holt of *that* story."

"Excepting it wouldn't do you much good anyways," Hoke said, "seeing as how you wouldn't be in a condition to read it except betwixt now and Saturday, unfortunately, being deceased thereafter."

"I reckon that's true enough. But I'd still like to hear tell of that deadly gun battle."

"Well, you ain't gonter, alas."

Hoke sat contentedly, less interested for the moment in the subject at hand than in his boots, which he believed he might replace with something in a soft, tooled calf. Meanwhile Dingus remained silent for a time. Then he interrupted Hoke's reverie to ask, "What you gonter do with all that reward money anyways, Hoke?"

Hoke had his old boots on the desk. "Ain't rightly thought," he said.

"Leastways you don't have to bear me that grudge no more, seeing as how you got your eight hundred dollars back. Way it turns out, you're about twenty-two hundred dollars to the good."

"I don't hold you no more grudge, Dingus. None a-tall. I reckon now it's your turn to hold one on me."

"You was jest doing your job, was all. Sheriff's a sheriff, even in bed. Sort of a unglorious way to get took though, in a feller's underdrawers."

"I ain't told nobody that aspect of it, Dingus."

"I appreciate that, Hoke."

Again Hoke was happy to see the subject drop. What he had failed to mention was that there must indeed have been a story about the capture, since several of the newspapers had long since written in request of his participant's version of the episode. Hoke had replied with laudable modesty in each case, if with a certain cloudiness of detail.

Meanwhile Dingus had arisen, stretching. He stood rubbing his neck with his left hand.

That reminded Hoke of something. "Say now, how come you ain't got no scar on your wrist there, from where you was all bandaged that time you robbed me?"

For a moment Dingus considered the wrist vacantly. Then he gestured in dismissal. "Oh, that—that weren't but a slight puncture, was all. I always did heal pretty quick anyways."

"You dint actually have it out with some peace officer, truly now? What I mean, not no authentic face-on gun shooting?"

"Weren't nothing," Dingus reiterated. "Couple fellers over to Tombstone, got a little rambunctious in a saloon one night and tried to draw down on me. Feller name of Earp, I believe it were, and one name of Holliday. Should of kilt 'em both, most probably, but I were in a sort of playful mood, so I jest poked 'em around with the butt end of a pistol, and then I—"

Hoke's jaw had fallen. "*Wyatt* Earp? And *Doc* Holliday?"

Dingus shrugged. "Same fellers, doubtless. I don't generally give such incidents too much notice, seeing as how they get to happening all the time. You know how it is, them little chaps trying to cut in on a bigger chap's reputation—"

Dingus actually yawned then, while Hoke continued to stare. "Sure never thought they'd swing me at only a tender nineteen and a quarter years," the youth went on.

"Happens that way, 'times," Hoke ventured, still impressed.

"Well, I had me some fun," Dingus decided.

"I reckon you done, all right."

"Seems a shame, though, jest when I were going right good. Year or so more, I could have got as notorious as the best, say like Billy the Kid hisself, maybe."

"Well, the Kid were jest luckier'n you, insofar as he got to murder more folks. But you're pretty notorious anyways."

"I'd still like to read me the story about that deadly gun battle," Dingus sighed. "Sort of a shame for you too, Hoke, when you stop to think."

"How you calculate?"

"Not getting but only three thousand dollars. You ought to have waited a spell to capture me. Dint they get ten thousand when they shot down the Kid, up to Fort Sumner?"

"Well, I reckon Pat Garrett's a luckier peace officer'n me,

same as the Kid were a luckier outlaw'n you," Hoke judged.
"But what's done is done, like they say."

"Don't rightly have to be, I reckon."

"How's that, now?"

"It jest come to me out'n the blue, Hoke, standing right
here in my stocking feet. Be right interesting if'n I escaped
from this here jail of yours. A couple months and I reckon
there'd be all sorts of new warrants on me, seeing as how I
don't believe I'd change my rascal's ways none. You capture
me again, say in a year, and doubtless you could collect a
whole ten thousand fer your strongbox that time."

Hoke Birdsill was gazing at him narrowly. "Say that
again?"

Dingus cocked the sombrero back on his fair head. "All
I'm informing you, Hoke, is that right now you got yourself
a holt of three thousand dollars, ain't you? Ain't no way they
can take it back, is there?"

This time Hoke did not reply. He had swung around in
his chair to squint at a tacked-up reward poster.

"*Reward for the capture of,* ain't that what it says?" Dingus
asked. "Don't say nothing about you need to get me hanged
in addition, does it?"

Hoke Birdsill stood up, nibbling his mustache.

"Ain't no rule says it can't go to more'n ten thousand,
neither," Dingus added.

"But supposing it's some other sheriff shoots you? Like
say Mister Earp again, or—"

Dingus shrugged. "Feller needs to take *some* risk to get
ahead in this world, I reckon. But you know for a fact I have
a fondness for Yerkey's Hole, especially with the attraction
of Belle's place to lure a man. On top of which, like you jest
said without even thinking on it—now that I been sentenced,
why, all you'd need next time, you'd murder me on sight."

Hoke Birdsill scowled and scowled, watching Dingus
watch him.

"How would be a good way to do it?"

"I could slug you, I reckon. I'd be gentle, nacherly, but
there oughter be a lump."

"I got a lump already, where I happened to bang my head in a outhouse this morning. Ain't nobody saw that one."

"Well, there you be, that's half the job done then. It's like a omen. So now all you got to do is lay low a spell, until I can appropriate a horse, and then you call out a posse and go west whilst I go east."

Hoke folded his arms, gazing at the cell door.

"I ain't never done nothing dishonest before," he decided next. "I ain't got the habit."

"You ain't never had ten thousand dollars to grab holt of, neither."

"How kin I be sure it'll get to ten thousand?"

"Supposing I took the notion to shoot up a whole town, one Wednesday? Or to rob me a train?"

"Rob one. Give me your sworn word of honor you'll rob a train."

"Got to travel a good ways north to do that, Hoke."

"Well, you jest come on back fast afterwards. I'm taking chances anyways."

"Hoke, you got my oath. And trains'll get a feller up to ten thousand faster'n anything."

Hoke was convinced. Hastily, with a furtive glance toward the street, he unlocked the cell. "There's always horses hitched down near Belle's," he whispered.

"Jest as soon's I climb into my boots," Dingus said. "I'll use the rear exit, I reckon."

Hoke watched him depart, then almost snatched up a shotgun to halt him again even as the rear door closed. "Earp?" he repeated. Hoke swallowed. Then he shook his head, since it was too late now anyway. "But I'll sure jest have to find him betwixt the bedsheets the next time round again also," he decided. He paced nervously for some minutes, tasting the wax from his mustache now. Then, carefully, he set his derby upside down upon a moderately clean spot on the floor, wrinkled his shirt with regret, and smudged gun oil across his cheek and ran, stumbling, toward the nearest saloon. "Dingus!" he shouted, bursting through the batwing doors. "He clobbered me good, boys, he made his escape!"

But whether it was his own outcry or the sound of the gunfire which brought the few drinkers up short he did not know. There were exactly four shots, with a pause between the first two and the last, in the direction from which he himself had just come. Hoke whirled in confusion.

"What's he shootin' at if'n he already done got loose?" someone asked.

And then Hoke knew. Clutching at the key ring in his vest with one hand, he clapped the other against his forehead, and the moan came from deep in his throat.

He was the first one back to the jail, but when he raced past the smashed door of the smallest cell and saw the fractured lock on his private strongbox beneath the cot, he did not even have to look into the box itself. He sank to his knees, burying his face into the mattress. "I might have knowed," he told himself, sobbing, "I might have knowed. And now probably he don't intend to go rob that train, neither!"

That was when the outrage had begun for C. L. Hoke Birdsill. It ran deep now, refulgent and intractable, as he stood in the alley behind the Yerkey's Hole livery stable six months later clutching the Smith and Wesson he had just emptied at the sight of that long-familiar and hateful Mexican vest, confronted by the sprawled form of a man who was not Dingus Billy Magee and not anyone else he had ever seen and whose name, he would learn, was Turkey Doolan. Hoke commenced to curse unremittingly.

There was gathering chaos about him now, however, and there were incalculably more people than the lone stable-hand with whom he had been talking when the shooting began, when he had heard the stablehand shout and had glanced up to see the fool he had taken for Dingus riding brazenly past the livery's rear doorway and had flung himself behind the nearest animal, snatching at his revolver— townspeople collecting, come in their cautious good time now that the firing was patently done with. Hoke cursed them also.

"*Who is it? Who'd Birdbrain go shooting this time?*"
"*Is it Dingus? Did he finally nail the critter?*"

"Fooled him again, I reckon."

"Say, I know that feller—jest a Missouri drifter, name of Rooster something—"

"Hoke done shot up some chickens, you say?"

Hoke gazed at Turkey, who had been lying beatifically for several moments now, since muttering some words about his comradeship with Dingus Billy Magee. And then abruptly the youth began to scream.

"It's stopped!" he cried. "The dripping's stopped! All my blood is dripped out! I'm kilt, I'm kilt!"

People were kneeling near him. "Easy now, easy," someone told him. "Hold him down, somebody!"

"Well, he sure ain't dead, anyways," Hoke said.

"I *am* dead!" Turkey screamed. "My blood is all dripped out! I could hear it dripping and now I can't!"

"Does look like he's lost a intolerable amount at that," a cowboy remarked. Hoke could see it now also. "Lying in a whole flood of it there—"

"I told you!" Turkey wailed. "And now there ain't no more to drip!"

"Can't be from this here wound in his side. This ain't nothing but a harmless crease."

"I doubt if'n I hit more than the once," Hoke said. "Durned forty-fours jest ain't no account fer accuracy."

"You think maybe he jest done peed in his pants with the fright of it?"

"I dint never pee!" Turkey cried. "I'm murdered!"

"Oh, thunderation, ain't blood. Ain't pee neither." A man had lifted something from beneath him. "Ain't nothing but his canteen been dripping here. It got punctured."

Turkey fainted on the spot.

"Somebody lug him down to the doc's," Hoke said. He did not assist them. He had lost his derby while shooting and he went to retrieve it now. Then, still outraged, he was striding toward the main street when someone called to him.

"Hey, Sheriff, look here—"

"I got work to do," Hoke snarled. "If that diaper-bottomed damn desperado thinks he can keep getting away with riding in here and making me shoot up innocent folks he's got another think coming. And I don't give a whorehouse hoot if'n he does face up to Wyatt Earp and the rest of them. I got to git back to my office and ponder what sort of mischief he's most likely got in mind. Because this time I'm gonter—"

"You better look at this here blood first, I reckon—"

"I already seen it. I been hearing enough about it too. All that commotion over a little bullet hole in the belly—"

"Not this. This ain't his'n."

"This ain't whose'n?"

"Here, where the second horse skittered afore it run off. Bring a lamp, somebody. This is too far aside to be that Turkey feller's."

Hoke gazed at the stains in the dim light. He ran his tongue across his mustache, which tasted faintly of gunpowder at the moment.

"What do you think, Hoke? You think maybe one of the five bullets that didn't hit the one you thought was Dingus and was aiming at might of hit the one you didn't think was, and wasn't?"

"Unless it's horse blood," someone else speculated.

"Ain't horse blood neither," Hoke said, "but either way he ain't going far, and that's the Lord's truth of it." He started off once more, then whirled anew. "And you're all witnesses to that blood now too," he said, "jest in case he crawls into a dung pile somewheres and dies, and somebody else goes picking up the remains and claiming them rewards. Because he's worked hisself all the way back up to nine thousand and five hundred dollars last I were informed, even without no train, and that money's mine!"

3

"When I play poker, a six-gun beats four aces."

Attributed to Johnny Ringo

Dingus, on the other hand, was mostly amused.

He had spurred his mount through a back trail to the far end of the town, and then he had almost fallen from the saddle, but even this failed to disturb him. "That Hoke," he told himself merely. "He gets into the habit of shooting folks he ain't pointing at and I'm gonter have to commence wearing that vest again myself."

He rested beneath a cottonwood tree while waiting for the blood to stop, which it did. It was full dark now, and not far away he could see a lamp burning within the doorway of a makeshift clapboard miner's shack. There was an odor of woodsmoke in the air, faintly tinged with kerosene and manure.

When he stood again he discovered he had bled a good bit down his right pantleg and into his boot. That sock was soggy, and he limped gingerly with his weight on the other foot. "Well, howdy do," he muttered. He kept one hand clasped over the wound, which pained him only slightly.

The shack was set apart from several others like it, amid tall weeds. There was no door, only a threadbare horse blanket hung from nails. Dingus considered this for a moment or two, then lifted the blanket and peered in.

The single room was dense with smoke from an untrimmed wick, and the faulty lamp itself stood on an upended wood crate. Beyond that Dingus saw a disreputable shuck mattress on the dirt floor, a half-finished tin of beans on an upturned nail keg with flies swarming around that, and some rag ends of clothing hung from pegs. Otherwise there was nothing in the rank room except the man himself, whom Dingus did not know. He doubted that he wanted to. The man was tall and gaunt, with a face like a hastily peeled potato, and he had only one arm, the right one. He was also completely bald.

"I'm ahurtin'," Dingus told him.

The man had been gazing emptily into the uneven, flickering glow of the lamp, and when he turned toward Dingus it was slowly, without surprise and without evident interest either. His long yellowed underwear was out at elbow and knee, spotted with savorings of a hundred meals. For a time he stood absently. Then his one arm lifted as if in accusation. "There's gonter be violence wrought upon this new Sodom," he intoned. "The wrathful fist of the Lord is gonter bring down fireballs and brimstone on it, sure as bulls has pizzles."

Dingus cocked his head in curiosity. The man scowled, preoccupied. Then he nodded. "It's whoredom," he said knowingly. "Whoredom and the barter of womanflesh, arunning rampant. The emissaries of Satan, that's what they be, and their name is women."

"I'm ahurtin' moderately bad," Dingus said.

But the man was brooding now, or perhaps he was somewhat deaf. He could have been Dingus's own age or twice that; with the light gleaming on his hairless narrow lumpy skull Dingus found it impossible to tell. "Gomorrah," the man muttered. "But like it come to them cities of the plain, so too's it gonter come to Yerkey's Hole, which is a turdheap and a abomination in the eye of the Lord. That's a fact, ain't it?"

"I ain't thought about it none," Dingus said, remotely interested now. So now the tall man merely belched.

"Womenflesh and womenwhores," he said, "but they ain't atricking Brother Rowbottom, even if'n my appointed mission ain't quite clear yet. Give me a dollar."

"It's got started throbbing some," Dingus remembered.

He was still holding one hand against the wound. "How far up the path there is the doc's?"

"The doc's?" The hand of the tall man rose and fell contemptuously. His voice was becoming more resonant now also. "A doc of the bones. I am a doc of the spirit, a doc of the soul. The wages of sin is Boot Hill, sure as sheep get buggered, but the way to salvation burns like a dose of clap. Ain't you got a lousy dollar to give me?"

"I reckon I'll find it myself, then," Dingus decided.

"Go then. But you're gonter regret it, same's all the rest, soon's I get the notification clear about my mission, oh yair." Abruptly the man whirled to settle himself onto the shuck mattress, pulling a mottled quilt about his trunk with his one arm. The activity revealed an upright whiskey jug at the wall. "Go," he muttered.

"Pleased to make your acquaintance," Dingus told him.

The man yanked the quilt over his head, turning aside. "Go on, scram," he repeated. "Beat it. See if I give a fart on a wet Wednesday."

Dingus shook his head, backing out. "Folks is right kindly," he told his horse, still holding himself. He began to draw the animal along a rocky path which led toward the main cluster of buildings.

It was a walk of some length, but he was still amused. He knew roughly where the doctor's would be, anyway, even approaching from the rear, and then a moon appeared, which helped.

But he had not yet achieved his destination when a dark squat figure loomed up to block his way. He was passing the fractured remains of an abandoned sutler's wagon, and he sprang against it, a hand jerking at one of his revolvers.

"You want bim-bam? Best damn bim-bam this whole town."

This time Dingus laughed aloud, releasing the gun. The squaw's thickly buttered hair gleamed dimly, and she stank of it. She was short and square-headed.

"You look for bim-bam, hey? Twenty-five cent, real hot damn bargain."

"I look for the doc's," Dingus said.

"Doc's? Why you look for there? You come scoot on around behind wagon, Anna Hot Water fix you up pretty damn nifty, better than that old doc. What for you hold onto yourself that way for anyhow, hey?"

But Dingus had limped past her, considering a row of adobe brick houses which fronted on the main street. "That's Doc's, ain't it—on up to the end there?"

"Maybe, sure, who care?" The squaw trundled after him. "You don't change your mind first, hey? You go to Big Blouse Belle's, pay whole damn dollar. Anna Hot Water, only damn independent bim-bam in town. Damn hot stuff too, you betcha. Twenty cent, maybe? Fifteen?"

Dingus left her, grimacing when the odor followed him for a time, although still laughing to himself. The pain had diminished almost wholly now. He led his horse into the doctor's small barn, easing its bit but not unsaddling the animal, before he crossed the silent sandy yard to knock at the rear door.

The doctor appeared almost at once, a short, elderly, scarcely successful but roguish-eyed man carrying a lamp that he raised for recognition's sake. That came immediately also. "Well," he said cheerfully, not quietly either, "if'n it ain't Dingus. Been expecting you, what with another of your chums just brought in. You come for your vest like always, I reckon?"

"I reckon. Only I also got a—"

"Well, come in, come in!" The doctor waved him into a familiar kitchen, turning to set aside the lamp. "I jest put that feller Turkey to sleep inside—nothing but a scratch, actually." He was dipping water into a coffee pot with a gourd, his back turned. "But you're gonter get one of them poor critters murdered yet, you know that, don't you?"

"Ah, Doc, you know Hoke—he couldn't hit nobody if'n he was shooting smack-bang down a stone well. Matter of fact he missed Turkey so bad tonight, durned if'n he dint go and—"

"Sit a spell," the doctor said, glancing across his shoulder. "You look a mite peaked yourself."

"Don't reckon I can," Dingus said.

"Can't what?"

"Can't sit," Dingus said. "What I been trying to tell you, about how Hoke ain't never gonter murder nobody. Shucks, he were aiming at Turkey all the while, but durned if'n the old blind mule-sniffer dint go and plink me square in the ass—"

"There some new preacher feller in town these days, Doc?" Dingus asked. He lay on his stomach on a leather couch, with his head raised as he tried to watch.

"Stop jiggling, there," the doctor told him. "If a man could get to see his own backside without he needed a mirror, I reckon maybe folks wouldn't get booted there so frequent as they do. What's that about a preacher?"

"Tall feller, bald as a bubble. Got only one arm."

"Oh, that's jest Brother Rowbottom. Can't say if'n he were ever ordained anywheres, but he does take himself for a preacher at that, if'n he can get anybody to listen. Talk about a good swift foot where it fits, he gets that from old Belle Nops pretty regular himself, seeing as how he's got the notion that the best place to tell folks about sin is where they's doing it. Goes pounding on up to the bordello and yammering the Lord's own storm about fornication and what all else, or fer as long as he can outrun Belle anyways. Don't do no harm, I judge. Hold on there, this might pain you some—"

Dingus pressed his jaws together, clutching the arm of the couch as the doctor probed. He released his breath slowly.

"Got it," the doctor went on. "I reckon it must of been spent a little, maybe deflected off'n your saddle first, or otherwise it would of torn right through. But this ain't critical a-tall." He crossed the room, removing something from a low cabinet. "Yep, Brother Rowbottom. Been around about a month now. Does a little pan mining too, I believe, though he ain't had much luck with it. Mostly he jest tickles folks." The doctor came back. "Won't be but a while longer—keep on lying still there. Come to think on it, we been getting a right smart of new folks in town of late. Even a new schoolteacher."

Dingus winced, tensing his cheeks at an unexpected sting. "I dint even hear tell there were a school," he said.

"Well, there weren't, until Miss Pfeffer chanced on along last month. She come out to marry up with some Army lieutenant over to Las Cruces, were the original of it, except the lieutenant drunk some alkali water about a week before she got here and up and died. You recollect that wood frame house Otis Bierbauer were building up the road here before that drunk Navajo bit him one night, and then it turned out the Navajo weren't drunk but had the rabies and we had to shoot the both of them? She moved in there. Right proper Eastern lady, a little horsy-looking in the face maybe, but a lip-smacking shape to her, even if'n it's all such virgin soil there's doubtless nine rows o' taters could be harvested under her skirts."

"Ain't no such animal," Dingus offered.

"Well, your chum Hoke Birdsill's sure found out otherwise. He's been courting to beat all, ever since she got here, without he had no more luck than a gelded jackrabbit. Sits up there in her parlor holding his derby hat on his knee is the all of it. But then Hoke's been in a bad fix over proper flesh to bed down for half a year now, ever since he apprehended you that one time and Belle cut him off from free poontang up to the house. That's how come he got hisself into trouble with that squaw to start with."

"I don't reckon I heard about that neither, Doc."

The doctor was trimming bandages with a Bowie knife, standing within Dingus's vision now, although he did not look up. "Pretty amusing, actually," he said. "She'd be a Kiowa from the square shape to her forehead, I'd judge, although most like she's got some mongrel strains to her too. Name's Anna Hotah or some such, but folks settles for Anna Hot Water and lets it go at that. Seems old Hoke got to be mighty tight with a dollar once you'd escaped him out of both his pimping job and that reward money to boot, which didn't leave him no more than his forty dollars a month from being sheriff, and so one day he rides off into the hills and he's gone for, oh, like onto a week, and when he gets back it develops he's got this squaw in tow. Comes in a bit battered and hangdog-looking also, like he's had a wearying time somewheres, but he don't say nothing about that. This were eight, ten weeks ago, I calculate, and he had the squaw living in a lean-to out back of the jail after that. But then like I say, Miss Pfeffer gets to town, and Hoke kicked out the squaw and commenced his courting. But poor old Hoke, Anna Hot Water ain't took to the idea so good yet. What I hear tell, she keeps tracking after him, calling him some right potent names and threatening to claim his scalp too, if'n he don't marry up with her. Causes Hoke a mite of embarrassment, you might say, specially what with his intentions toward Miss Pfeffer."

"I reckon," Dingus laughed. The doctor was wiping his hands.

"You can hoist your trousers back on, lad. You in the mood for a snort?"

"I'd be obliged. What kin I pay you, Doc?"

"Oh, weren't complicated. Dollar be adequate." The doctor lifted a bottle from a desktop, holding it while Dingus adjusted his buckles. "But speaking of gossip, I hear tell you been up to some shenanigans of late yourself."

"No more'n usual, I reckon. But meantimes you ain't never gonter manage to retire on jest a lone dollar, Doc—"

"Oh, a man don't hardly make a living for fifty years, he gives up on it eventually. But no, what I hear, they got you posted all the way back up to nine thousand or more in rewards, now."

Dingus took the bottle, nodding thoughtfully. "You know, Doc, I'm hanged if'n I don't hear the same thing. But it's right peculiar, too. Because to speak the Lord's truth, I've been sort of behaving myself most currently. Oh, I done a few harmless little pranks here and there, but they never added up to more'n four thousand and five hundred dollars in bounty on me, and that's a true fact. But then last month I find there's a whole five thousand more dollars on top of that, and durned if'n I weren't all the way down to Old Mex when them last ones happened. Looks like if a feller gets a mite of a reputation they'll hold him in account fer everything, even if'n he's tending to his own business somewheres else."

"Well now, that's jest one of the penalties of fame, I reckon." The doctor disappeared into the next room, and when he returned he carried the vest and the sombrero. "Blood's dried," he said, "but the bullet hole's up under the arm this time—won't show so proudly as these earlier ones."

"Turkey still sleeping in there?"

"I give him a strong dose, since he turned out the nervous kind. Peed all over my kitchen table when I went to work on him. You got somewheres you're gonter hole up, Dingus? You won't be able to ride none, not for a couple of days, and even then you'd best have a pillow in the saddle."

Dingus was buckling into his guns. "There's places, I reckon."

"Beats me why you come back on in here so frequent anyways, what with Hoke all riled up about you the way he's been."

"I got me some special plans this time."

"Well, you better wait on them until you can ride. I'd let you stay here, except there's a limit to the law-breaking a man can do, even if'n he does happen to be a medical doctor."

"Don't fret youself, Doc." They were at the door. "Lissen, you don't mind, I'd favor to leave my horse out there in your barn for a spell."

"You young studs," the doctor said.

Unhurriedly, Dingus crossed the yard to unsaddle and feed his mount. When he emerged from the barn he was carrying his Winchester in one hand and his shotgun in the other. He was whistling when he retraced his steps along the path he had followed earlier.

So he did not quite have to reach the overturned wagon this time before she materialized out of its shadows. "You want bim-bam? Best damn bim-bam this whole damn town."

The idea had come to him in the barn, and he chuckled softly. "Howdy," he said.

"Oh, sure, you come back, hey? Change your mind like smart feller. Twenty-five cent, cash in advance."

"Ain't that," Dingus said, smelling her once more. "Turns out I'm in rotten shape anyhow."

"How come is that? That old Doc, he no fix you up so good? I told you, stay with Anna Hot Water, she fix you up real damn neat."

"I hear tell you acquainted with Sheriff C. L. Hoke Birdsill. That a fact?"

"That a fact, okay. That son-um-beetch. He marry me pretty damn quick, you betcha, or I fix him pretty damn quicker."

"I hear tell he ain't gonter marry you a-tall. What I hear, he's gonter marry that there schoolteacher, Miss Pfeffer."

"Hey, where you hear that? That son-um-beetch, I fix him quick, he try that."

"Well, I hear it for a gen-u-ine fact, all right." Talking, Dingus had set the shotgun against the tilting wagon. Now he shrugged. "Well, I'm gonter be moseying on."

"That son-um-beetch," Anna Hot Water said. Dingus had started away. "Hey, you in rotten shape okay, I think. You don't even remember your shotgun here."

"I'm right sick," Dingus said, not turning back. "I don't reckon I can even carry it no more."

"Hey?" Anna Hot Water said.

"Be a right fancy wedding, Hoke and that there schoolteacher," Dingus said. He left it with her, whistling again.

So he was truly amused now, and when the rest of it occurred to him he actually had to stop and press a hand over the wound as he laughed. "Why, surely," he told himself. "Especially since I got to put off what I come for anyways."

He had to cross the main street, and lights blazed in several saloons, but no one was about. He did not hurry. Farther down he could see lamps beyond several of Belle's upper windows also.

He found the house easily enough, still grinning, but then he paused in the brush behind it to stand for a time quite thoughtfully, blowing into a fist. There were no lights here. "But we know you're in there, Miss Pfeffer, ma'am," he said aloud. "Jest alaying in your lily bed and dreaming juicy dreams about old Hoke, ain't you? So now how are we gonter manipulate this in the most guaranteed and sure-fire way? Why nacherly, we'll jest take a lesson from Hoke hisself . . ."

So when the light came into the doorway in answer to his knock, all four of his revolvers and his Winchester were well hidden in the sage, and he himself was huddled against the railing of the narrow plank porch, his arms pressed into his stomach. His hair was disheveled, and his shirt was torn, and there was dirt smeared across his face. "Please!" he cried, and there was a whimper of anguish in his voice, "oh, please, help me, help me—"

"Who's there? What—"

"Please, ma'am!" Dingus staggered toward the indrawn door, lifting his face plaintively to the light. "Outlaws! I need help bad. I been hurt—"

"Why, you *are* hurt. And you're just a boy—"

"Yes'm. If I could only come inside."

He managed to slip past her in her confusion, stumbling toward a table and bracing himself there with his head hanging again. He commenced to pant.

"But what is it? Do you need a doctor? Should I—"

"They're after me! The door! Please, oh please, out of Christian charity—"

"But I don't—"

The door closed, however, perhaps because he had turned to confront her again, once more with his face screwed into a grimace of terror and plaintiveness (although he was seeing the woman herself finally now also, the mouse-colored hair in curl papers, the long blunt equine jaw, the plain dull disturbed expression above the drab nightrobe, so that even as he continued to feign desperation he was already thinking, "Well, Doc dint tell me any lie about her looks, but at least she ain't built bad a-tall"). "Thank you," he gasped. "The good Lord will bless you for this kind deed done for a boy in distress."

"But what is it? What's—"

He let his breath become regular, straightening himself somewhat. "Badmen," he declared with gravity then. "They shot my old cripped daddy, kilt him dead, and now they're after me because I seen their faces and can be a witness. They shot me too, only I can't tell you where. What I mean, it's sort of delicate, being my backside—"

"Oh, you tragic boy. But I don't see any blood. Is it—"

"No," he said quickly, "that were earlier. I got that patched up, but then I saw them again and now they're hunting me. Like fiends. In the town here."

"But the sheriff—shouldn't you go to Sheriff Birdsill?"

"Oh, no, no—" Dingus lifted a hand imploringly. "That's jest what they expect me to do, so they'll be watching over that way, do you see? But I'd be safe from harm's way here, if'n you've got a floor for me to rest on—only 'til dawn, and then I'd slip away and never intrude upon your goodness again. You'd be saving a wretched orphan's life, ma'am."

Miss Pfeffer kept glancing toward the door, concerned for him but still dubious, so he lurched away from her then and staggered toward a farther room, clutching at the doorframe for support. "Oh, but it pains me so!" he sobbed.

"Oh, dear me—" Miss Pfeffer sprang after him. "Yes, you dear child, lie down, use my bed there, it's—"

"Oh, no ma'am, you're too kind. Any old place on the floor will do me . . ." Dingus sagged into her arms.

"But you *are* hurt! Here, I insist!"

So he let himself be led to the already turned-back bed, tumbling across it. He lay on his side, with his feet over the edge. "My boots," he sighed. "I jest ain't got the strength to—"

"Here, here, let me—" Miss Pfeffer set down her lamp, kneeling to the first of them. It came free easily, exposing the soggy, bloodstained sock. "Oh!" Miss Pfeffer cried. "Oh, it's all—"

"Yes'm. I lost considerable amounts before I got to the doc."

"Oh dear! Dear me!" She removed the other boot, rising to hold it in consternation. The color had drained from her long face, such color as there had been. "Your clothes. Do you think you ought to—"

"Yes'm, I'd rest far more comfortable. Only"—Dingus blushed, lowering his eyes—"I'd take it right kindly if'n you'd leave. I can manage, I'm sure I can—"

Miss Pfeffer's own face was averted. "But you'll call me, if you're too ill—"

"Yes'm."

He undressed leisurely then, hearing her pace elsewhere in the house. Now and then she mumbled something. When he extinguished the lamp, calling out to her, she pranced back into the room anxiously.

"I hope you'll forgive the lamp being off without your permission," Dingus started then. "But my daddy would think badly of me, if'n I were lacking my proper clothing in a lady's presence without the light was out. Oh, my poor daddy—" Dingus commenced to sob. "Right before my very eyes, this very day, they shot him down like a dog, and I won't never kiss his dear furrowed brow again—"

So Miss Pfeffer hovered above him now. "You unfortunate soul. How did it happen? Will it help you to talk about it?"

Dingus sobbed and sobbed. "It were rustlers. They took our cattle, even every last helpless little calf that my daddy toiled so hard to care for. And then they set fire to our ranch, too, that my daddy homesteaded with the sweat of his tired, lame shoulders. Oh, it were jest unbearable!"

A hand stroked his own in commiseration. "And to think they would take up arms against someone of your age!" Miss Pfeffer shuddered. "But your mother, don't you have a—"

"Oh," Dingus wailed, "don't make me talk about my mother, please! That were too sad, I still can't think about it without I start to weep worse'n ever!" The hand bad started to lift; Dingus clutched at it desperately. "And it's all the more sadder here, too, because you remind me of her. Not that you're anywheres near as old as her, but jest that you're beautiful the same way. And kind, too, and refined. But then those dreadful Comanches come, and they dragged her out into the fields, and they bound her to four stakes in the ground, and then they—" Dingus emitted a choked gasp. "But it ain't a fit thing to relate before a woman. It were God's pure mercy that she died within the month. I weren't but eleven . . ."

"Dear heaven! And now you're all alone—"

"All alone on God's earth, yes'm. But I'm safe here. Only—"

"Yes, what is it?"

"I'm so cold. All of a sudden, my wound hurts right bad, and I feel this terribe chill. I can't hardly keep from shivering."

"Wait, here, let me—"

Dingus felt the additional blankets being spread across him. "But them must be what you would of slept with yourself," he protested, shaking now. "I c-c-couldn't take y-y-yours."

"Oh, dear, it *is* bad, isn't it?"

"Yes'm. I sure wish I had a brother or some kin here. My mommy always used to tell me that were the only way to stop a ch-ch-chill, to sleep all huddled up close to your brother. Excepting it were Apaches that kilt *him*. When I were nine. They—they—"

Dingus shivered and shivered. "Oh, heavens," Miss Pfeffer said in the darkness, talking as if to herself now. "Oh dear me. But I must, yes. It is only charitable. Christian. I must—"

He waited until he was certain, hearing the rustling. Then he cried, "Ma'am, ma'am, what are you *doing!*"

"Hush now. That chill could be the death of you."

"Oh, I know that, ma'am. I could go to my reward before the night is past, I don't doubt that I could. But I done stripped down completely out'n my—"

"But that's how it must be done." Dingus felt the blankets being drawn aside, waiting without a move as she drew him into her embrace. "Of course," she said, "you feel feverish too. Indeed. I think perhaps if you would turn over, then I could cover you more fully."

"Oh, dear," Dingus said. "Is that the only way it will save

me? Because I can't stay nohow but on my stomach, alas, what with this wound I got. Would it work to keep me warm the same way if'n I was the one who climbed on the—"

"Yes, I believe so. It's the transference of the body's heat which is important. Here. Wait, and I'll—"

"This sure is a kindness, ma'am. I'm feeling consider-able warmer already. But I'm right embarrassed too. What I mean, I've never been in the same bed with a female person, of course, but isn't this how—I mean the way—I mean—"

"Heavens, I don't know either. Do you think this is all that—"

"Well, I certainly never expected *you* would know, ma'am, not a respectable unmarried lady like yourself. But what I would guess, it probably has got something to do with—well, not meaning anything, but jest sort of hypothetical, I reckon I would have to adjust my position a trifle, sort of like this—I mean if I were growed up enough and we were married folks and all, which is the only circumstances under which I would give a passing thought to such things . . ."

"Of course. But hypothetically, yes, if we were, do you imagine it's anything like—"

"Well, this could be it, maybe. But next I would most likely have to arrange myself like this, and then sort of like . . ."

"Like *that?*"

"I reckon so. And then I'd—"

"Oh, dear. Oh, dear me—"

"Don't you reckon that would be how it—"

"Well, I don't *know,* but—but—"

"Oh. Oh, well, hang it now—"

"What is it? What are you doing? Oh, don't! Please don't, I—"

"Well, now, I jest can't help it, ma'am, I truly can't. Durned if'n that chill ain't come back over me, worse'n ever. Why, I jest think I'm about to start shivering so I can't stop for nothing—"

Perhaps he heard her. In any event he dozed only fit-fully, vaguely conscious that she was pacing. Moonlight was streaming through a window then, and later he would definitely recall a vision of her standing over him, wringing her hands. "What have we done?" she was wailing. "What have we *done!*" But then he turned away from the disturbance.

Or perhaps he saw her when she was dressing also, or heard her when she decided, talking only to herself. "I'll have to ask someone," she said. "Because there must be a man of the cloth in town, surely. The sheriff would know. Yes, I'll ask Mr. Birdsill." But if he heard he gave no sign.

Yet when the pain woke him he seemed to know instinctively, knew even before he became aware that the blankets were coarser now, the bed more lumpy. What told him first was the ache itself, which was in his temple. Then, when he lifted a hand to touch the soreness, he knew without question, since his other hand was jerked upward by the movement, fixed fast to the first by the ancient rusted iron manacles.

He was in his woolens, but he could see his clothing where it lay in a pile on the cell floor. He found the tender lump behind his ear then too, and he moaned once, less in realization of his new predicament than from ineffable, sad resignation. "Oh, Dingus, you jest never ought to have gonter sleep," he said aloud.

"I don't reckon you should of," Hoke Birdsill said indulgently.

Dingus was on his right side, and he turned his head experimentally, considering Hoke through the bars. The sheriff sat at his all-too-familiar desk, evidently writing something, and a shotgun was situated at his right hand, pointing directly into the cell. "Nice to have you back, you double-dealing, women-and-children-terrifying dishonorable skunk," Hoke said, setting aside the pen.

So Dingus felt it then himself, finally began to taste the beginning of an outrage of his own. He started to sit up, forgetting about his wound, and then had to jerk back quickly as the pain caught him up. Hoke laughed. "You feeling somewhat peaked, are you, you miserable twerp?"

"I feel all right," Dingus grunted. "No thanks to you, you boudoir-crawling varmint. Goldang it now, every durned time a feller takes off his pants you—how'd you get me in here? You found me asleep and went and pistol-whipped me, dint you, you—"

"Weren't nothing," Hoke said casually. "Although as it happens I were jest writing the facts of it down, on account of the newspapers will no doubt be interested."

"You gonter tell me, or jest sit there licking that floppy yeller mustache?"

"Why, sure, but like I say, it weren't nothing. Miss Agnes Pfeffer come rushing in here, oh, maybe half an hour back, all distracted and talking about a preacher or some such, and so first I thought maybe it were a feller in town, name of Brother Rowbottom, raising a small ruckus somewheres like he does. But then she remarked about it being a boy all shot up, and so I dint have to ask what boy, not being a famous peace officer jest because of my handsome good looks alone, nacherly. So anyways I dint let her rave no more, but I told her who you was, and then that poor helpless creature, why, she like to scared me out'n my wits with a heartrending fainting fit. Goes to show you what being confronted with a immoral desperado like yourself will do to a well-bred lady, all right. Which reminds me that Doc has no doubt took her back home by now, and I ought to go on up and reassure her that you're permanently out'n harm's way once again in your degenerate career. I already done finished writing *that* letter, incidentally, asking when I kin get to put a rope around your miserable neck again, and the one to Santa Fe about that nine thousand and five hundred dollars in the new rewards likewise. Meantimes don't start thinking you're gonter trick me about escaping no second time, Dingus, not with them handcuffs and—"

"Did I ask you about all that? Did I ask you any blasted thing more than except how you got me in here?"

"Well, that were the all of it, anyways. After I took Miss Pfeffer to Doc's I jest went on up to her residence and apprehended you."

Dingus had raised himself to his hands and knees on the cot. "Well, fry your ornery hide—and I were asleep, weren't I? So what did you have to go and coldcock me for in the process?"

"Why, Dingus, whatever give you the idea you was asleep? You was a mite drunk, I reckon, seeing as how you'd done took your clothes off after the lady ran out, but you was parading around the house with your six-guns all primed and strapped on under your nekked belly-button, sure enough."

"Huh? Why, my guns wasn't nowheres near the—"

"'Course they was. And then we drawed on each other, like always happens when a stalwart sheriff meets up with a notorious desperado—but I beat you easy. Had the drop on you afore you could scratch two gnats off'n a whore's behind. So then you tried to skedaddle, being cowardly at heart like most immoral criminals. I could of kilt you, but I dint see no reason to do that, seeing as how I get the same reward money either way. So I jest calmly shot you on a tangent, like, in a location where you couldn't run too fast, is all."

Dingus howled at him, charging to the front of the cell. "Why, you—you—is that what you're saying done happened?"

"Reckon so, especially seeing as how I jest wrote it that way."

"Why, you coyote-brained, pussle-gutted, limp-tooled old polecat!" Dingus was sputtering. "Now blast it all, Hokc, I were shot in the ass long afore you ever snuck on into Miss Pfeffer's, and you know that for a gen-u-ine true fact!"

Hoke pursed his lips, eyeing him. "Now Dingus," he said. "You think a famous law officer like C. L. Hoke Birdsill has got time to fret over *details?*"

4.

---

*". . . the best job that was ever offered to me
was to become a landlord in a brothel.
In my opinion it's the perfect milieu
for an artist to work in."*

William Faulkner

So Hoke was content again, almost euphorically so. Because it had been a long and dismal six months, more full of frustration and bitterness than he wanted to remember.

Nor was Hoke thinking merely of that disastrous pretended jailbreak which had cost him both his reward money and his sinecure at Belle's, since that had only been a beginning. After that there had still been the duplicity of the vest for him to endure, if not to say almost becoming a murderer over—not only tonight with Turkey Doolan but twice before. Even now, as he smirked over his ultimate victory, the memory of those earlier misdirected shootings still brought a taste of gall to Hoke's mouth.

Both episodes had occurred very soon after Dingus tricked him. Hoke had taken instinctively to hanging around Belle's again, in the hope that he might redeem at least part of the calamity by getting his original job back, but Belle would not hear of it. As a matter of fact she had finally added insult to injury by ordering him to keep away from the bordello altogether unless he had money to spend.

So he was actually moping disconsolately outside the

house one night—wistfully eyeing Belle's own prohibited upper rear doorway, in fact—when the first of the new indignities befell him. Two riders appeared along a rarely used trail, and before Hoke quite knew what he was doing he had emptied his Smith and Wesson at one of them. The second rider spurred off, but Hoke could not have cared less—until he discovered that the man he'd hit, the man in the red-and-yellow fringed Mexican-wool vest, was an inconsequential saddle tramp named Honig. The tramp had suffered a mild gash in the hip. What Hoke himself suffered at the realization of this new treachery was hardly endurable.

So he began to spend time behind the bordello deliberately after that, well-hidden in a grove of cottonwoods and no longer even caring that he was further alienating Belle by being there. In fact he virtually camped in the trees for eight days, or more precisely nights, until Dingus cantered up along the same trail once again. This time it developed that he had presented the vest to a down-at-the-heels prospector named Arden. Hoke had set out three revolvers on a dry pine stump, and his third shot from the second gun nicked the prospector in the shoulder, going away.

So by then the outrage was more than unappeasable: Hoke was almost mad. Belle actually threatened to shoot him on sight if she caught him within a hundred yards of her premises now—as did one of her better customers likewise, an elderly, normally undemonstrative barber who had suffered a mild stroke in the arms of a twelve-year-old Mexican girl while Hoke was blasting away at the vest for the second time, yet Hoke ignored both threats. In fact he was even starting to construct a semi-permanent lean-to shelter in the trees before the doctor finally managed to calm him down somewhat.

Reluctantly Hoke let himself be talked into returning to the more banal routines of his office. But then it did seem most sensible to wait anyhow, since, abruptly, new warrants on Dingus began to cross his desk with gratifying frequency. In quick succession the youth was accused of stopping a Wells Fargo stage, of emptying a bank, of removing the contents of a safe in a freight office. Little more than a month after his escape, he was worth exactly fifteen hundred dollars more than he had been the last time.

Then, just as suddenly, all this ceased. Ordinary circulars came in as usual, but no more concerning Dingus. The price on his head held fast at four thousand five hundred dollars for the next three full months.

So Hoke was more than anxious again. And when he finally heard a rumor that Dingus had been seen in a town named Fronteras, some three days' ride from Yerkey's Hole, he oiled his Smith and Wesson, two Colt .45 Peacemakers, a Buntline Special, a shotgun, and a repeating Winchester, and he rode off.

He didn't find Dingus. He almost did not find the town either, since its mines had played out a year before and it had been summarily abandoned, at least by its builders. It had never numbered more than a dozen structures to start with, and now a motley gathering of displaced Indians was camped near its wells. Hoke had not even unsaddled when a short, square-headed, foul-smelling squaw whom he took to be at least part Kiowa approached his horse.

"You want bim-bam, hey? Only damn bim-bam two-day ride any direction."

Hoke ignored her, although she gave him an idea. In the four months since Belle Nops had fired him he had earned a grand total of one hundred and sixty dollars as sheriff. He was still living at the jail, but food alone had cost him almost a dollar a day for some hundred and twenty days. Hoke commenced to study the females in the tawdry encampment.

Several of them appealed to him. They were fairly young, and Hoke knew that they would not be married, since there were no buck warriors in evidence (he hardly would have stayed if there had been). He sought out the chief, an ancient, gnarled creature with a head startlingly flattened at the back from having been strapped too tightly to a cradle-board decades before, and with a face that had weathered into a mask of sewn leather. Hoke made his offer. "These here two Colt revolvers," he said, not wanting to part with what meager cash he did possess, "or the nice hand-tooled Buntline."

But the chief could only gaze at him vapidly, not understanding English. He was eating something which Hoke made out to be an unskinned wood rat, evidently boiled. Even before Hoke could seek her out then, the squaw who had stopped him initially again materialized at his side. "Why you trade for bim-bam, hey? You take Anna Hot Water, she come for free. Sick and tired, live with all these damn savages anyways. Anna Hot Water fix you up pretty damn nifty, sure hey?"

Most of the thirty-odd people in the encampment had gathered near them in curiosity, and Hoke had already settled on a thin girl of no more than thirteen, who appeared cleaner than most. "That there one," he pointed. "Tell the chief them's real accurate Colts, too."

"Ah, listen, Anna Hot Water plenty better for you than those damn baby bim-bams, no yes? Plenty experience, even married one damn time. Hey?"

Hoke fumbled in a vest pocket and came up with a silver dollar. "Here," he said, "I'll pay you, you put it into a lingo he can savvy. That skinny one over there, tell him."

Anna Hot Water tested the coin first on her teeth, then shrugged and commenced to speak, gesturing frequently. The young girl blushed, but the chief remained sullen, still gnawing on the rat. Finally he muttered something, nodding toward Hoke and then toward Hoke's mount.

"Chief say you stick lousy old Colts up you know where," Anna Hot Water interpreted. "He take Winchester repeater rifle, damn sure. And he say your loco hat too, hey."

Hoke frowned, briefly contemplative. The derby was not his best, however, and he finally removed it. He also lifted the Winchester from its scabbard. Then he motioned for the girl to follow, turning to mount but suddenly the chief had begun to mumble again.

"What's that, now?" Hoke asked.

"Tribal custom," Anna Hot Water explained. There were seven or eight birch wickiups in the encampment, and several tepees, and she indicated one of the latter. "Chief say not enough you pay, you got to prove you make good husband. You go into wigwam, you unbutton old Sitting Bull, and when him standing, girl she come in too. She not happy, you lose girl."

Hoke raised an eyebrow. "Huh?"

Then he saw that several old men, carrying rifles of their own, were eyeing him threatfully. "Oh, now look here," he said, "first off, it's broad daylight, and I ain't never remark-ably interested unless'n it's dark. And anyways I—"

"You be pretty damn interested I think," Anna Hot Water said. "Because if first girl no happy, chief send in second. If second say bum job, send third. Because it got to be fair trade, and it damn sure he not give back Winchester. He keep send in girls until one say okay."

"But what if'n none of them—I mean if'n it ain't satisfac-tory at the beginning it sure ain't gonter get to be more so after two or three or—"

"There seventeen bim-bam here, you betcha," Anna Hot Water said, "not count four old squaws of chief. You better be the hot stuff one time out of seventeen, or chief maybe forget about be fair, just shoot you pretty damn quick. Chief say man can't get it up one time in seventeen ought to be shot anyways, hey?"

"But this ain't sporting," Hoke protested. "You jest can't expect a man to—"

But he was actually being prodded toward the tepee now, the guns at his back, and then he discovered he was being undressed also, although he tried to fight it. "Lissen, be care-ful there, that coat come all the way from St. Louis by mail ordering. And anyways I been in the saddle for three whole days. I'm plumb tuckered out, and a man can't never—"

He was stripped to his stockings before being pushed through the entrance, roughly enough so that he went to his hands and knees. And then he saw that four women, very old and with faces even more deeply rutted than the chief's whose wives they probably were, were following him inside. They circled the perimeter of the tepee and then proceeded to take seats, crosslegged, on scattered skins. "Hey," Hoke called, "hey, now look—"

Hoke clapped a hand over his privates and whirled away, only to blush at what the new perspective revealed. The women sat grinning toothlessly.

"But—but—you ain't gonter stay in here too? You don't expect a man to perform his functions like he's a actor on a stage, or—"

But the first girl had appeared by now also, the one he had chosen. She began to giggle. Hoke lunged toward the entrance.

The rifles drove him back. Still giggling, the girl was disrobing then, nor were there undergarments beneath her buckskins. Hoke clapped his unoccupied hand across his eyes.

The old women commenced to titter now also, as he stood hopping from foot to foot.

Hoke finally heard moccasins scuffing, indicating that the girl had given up. "Okay, hey," Anna Hot Water said from the entry, "is one in, one out, pretty damn quick for tall nutsy feller like you, you betcha."

Hoke moaned, turning to glare from one of the old wives to another. "Now blast it all, how am I supposed to—"

But then another girl appeared, giggling even as she disclosed her respectable bosom. This time Hoke flung himself against the ridgepole of the tepee, pressing his face into the crook of his arm. "I can't!" he cried. "A man jest can't!"

"Is two in, two out, and not even one damn hard on," Anna Hot Water called. "But lots more damn time."

But now he did not even turn when the next girl entered, so after she had stripped herself one of the grinning old women reached across and thwacked him on the thigh with a stick. "I won't," Hoke said. "I won't!" He saw the girl, however, if only because of the increasing force of the blows, which finally made him dance away. But then as a fourth candidate was entering he threw himself to the ground, pounding at it with his fists.

The old women grinned and tittered, and he might have

seen a fifth girl, and even a sixth (noticing obliquely, if he noticed anything at all, that they became progressively less attractive, less young) but after that he not only ignored the smarting of the blows but the yanking at his hair also, and when his head was jerked forcibly upward he squeezed his eyes tight. "Take it," he was sobbing. "Take the durned rifle. Take the hat. Take the Colts too, and my horse. Jest don't send in no more. It jest ain't sporting. A man could go plumb out'n his—"

So he had no idea how long it took. When he at last became aware that he was alone, light through the entrance told him that not too much time could have passed after all. His clothing lay in a disorderly heap near him. He dressed slowly, vanquished, oblivious of the dirt on his garments.

His horse remained where he had left it, and his saddle gear likewise. The Indians, evidently all of them, were sitting in a half-circle, facing him, and he could read nothing in their expressions. The few old men with rifles held them approximately in his direction still. The four old wives sat indifferently to one side, picking lice from one another's hair.

"Okay," Hoke said, "so I couldn't. So I dint. Go ahead then, if'n that's your custom, shoot me and git it done with. But I reckon you could paint up a notice or something, to tell a feller he'd best coax it up in advance, afore he—"

The chief grunted in irritation, gesturing toward Hoke's horse. "He say take your squaw and scram," Anna Hot Water told him.

"Huh?" Hoke said.

"Chief say paleface usually pretty damn lousy at bim-bam anyways, but you the most miserable he ever got rifle from. Pretty lucky, you find some manhood in time to keep bargain, hey?"

"I done?" Hoke said. "But I never even—"

The chief grunted again, as if in dismissal, so Hoke edged toward the horse, although still totally confused. Then he realized that she had risen to follow after him.

"We get to civilization, you marry me pretty damn quick, I think," she said then. "Because it cost me that whole damn silver dollar, bribe old hags in teepee there. But oh, lover, you got yourself hottest damn bim-bam this whole territory, oh yes, hey!"

And there seemed no way to get rid of her. She had a pony, remarkably old and erratically gaited, but capable somehow of keeping in sight of his own roan when he tried to outrun her. "What for you want to do that anyways, hey?" she asked him reasonably. "I save your life back that stinking place, no? How quick we get married, yes?"

"Sure," Hoke said. "All right. Whatever suits you. I done give up on all hope back there anyways. But wash that smelly bear fat out'n your hair."

This was the first night, after they had camped near an arroyo through which a stream ran. "And while you're at it scrub down your durned clothes too," he told her.

"And then you have nice clean bim-bam, hey? Sure, must want it pretty damn bad, after seventeen times you don't get it. One feller, he come through there, decide to trade horse for squaw—he test all them women, twenty damn hours non-stop. Then all of them tell chief he too damn something, too, not want to be wife or be burned out in three weeks probably. Like make bim-bam with repeater rifle. And then chief have to give back horse damn fast himself, because old wives get hot fer feller too. This before I get stuck up there, but they still talk about it, oh yes. Feller named Dean Goose, I hear tell. That some hung feller, you betcha. Greatest bim-bam of all!"

Hoke rolled dismally into his blanket. "Feller named what?"

"Dean Goose."

Hoke sobbed once.

"That remind me, what your names, lover hey?"

Hoke did not answer.

"Well, I think I call you Dean Goose anyways, maybe that make you better bim-bam. You want bim-bam now, Dean Goose?"

"I'm right weary," Hoke sobbed.

"Sure, Dean Goose. We got plenty damn time, you betcha. Whole damn life I think."

But he finally got an idea the next afternoon. Their trail crossed the route followed by a stage line, and he picked a spot on a rise below which the road snaked for a substantial distance around a fully visible horseshoe curve. He said nothing to Anna Hot Water at all, gave no indication why they were camping in midafternoon. Nor did he explain when they sat there two days and nights.

When he finally saw a coach, perhaps five minutes away and coming fast, he strode quickly to where Anna Hot Water's pony was hobbled and put a bullet through the animal's head. The squaw leaped toward him. "Hey, what for you damn fool do that, hey?"

"He had that there limp."

"Hey, that no limp. He gaited that way long time now, damn good pony."

But Hoke was already mounting up. "He wouldn't of never got to California," he said.

"California? Hey, that where we go?"

"Dint I tell you? Sure, and now we'll have to find you another horse. Or say, ain't this some luck, because here comes a stage. I'll jest run on down and stop her, and then you can ride and I'll foller along after—"

"Hey?" Anna Hot Water said.

"Sure. And I reckon you never rode in no stagecoach before, neither. Git on down there quick, now."

Hoke galloped off. There was no trail where he angled toward the road below, and his horse skidded several times, raising dust, but with the instinct of his years as a cowhand he yanked his kerchief about his mouth and nose. It had already occurred to him that a stage might not make an unscheduled stop in Indian country, but he had decided that his personal emergency would warrant halting it with a gun. Because he truly meant to buy a ticket for as far away from Yerkey's Hole as his last few dollars would take her.

But then the coach surprised him by pulling up even before he had done any more than wave with his Buntline.

As a matter of fact it seemed the driver had begun to brake before that, when he had still been slipping down the hillside.

"Howdy there," Hoke shouted from a distance, heeling toward them. "I thank you kindly—"

But then they were to puzzle him even more. Because there were no passengers, apparently, and of the two men in the cockpit only one looked like an ordinary hand. The other, who should have been carrying a shotgun, was not only unarmed but quite elderly, and far too handsomely dressed for his situation. It was he who began to shout:

"Don't kill us! Don't! We're carrying nothing—no mail, nothing. Here's my wallet! There's three hundred dollars in it, and—"

"But—"

And then the man actually did toss a wallet toward him. Hoke gaped at it where it dropped into the dirt. "But I jest wanted to—"

The older man clutched at his breast then, gasping. "Oh, don't shoot!"

"But look, I'm jest trying to tell you—"

"Lissen, mister, lissen." It was the driver this time, leaning down to speak almost confidentially. "That's all we got with us, honest. This here's Mr. Fairweather, the owner. He's jest taking a private ride, you see. And he's got this weak heart, so I'm under orders not to put up no resistance. So if—"

"Well, sure," Hoke said. "Anyways, all I want is—"

Still confused, Hoke happened to lift a hand to his face. That was when he realized he had not put away his revolver. Nor had he removed his kerchief.

So he was just about to rid himself of both, grimacing at his stupidity, when the rest of it happened. Anna Hot Water came panting along the trail behind them. "What you say?" she called. "It all set now, Dean Goose?"

"Dean Goose?" the driver muttered. "Dean Goose?"

"Dingus Billy Magee!"

Hoke's horse shied at the abrupt lurching of the vehicle,

rearing high. Probably he could have caught them if he tried, but he was still simply not thinking well. "Yaaaa!" the driver screamed. "Yaaaa!" The coach jerked and skidded, rocking wildly down the road.

So the new circular on Dingus reached his office only a day after he himself got home (with Anna Hot Water plodding inexorably after him). It was for three thousand dollars, posted by an organization named the Fairweather Transportation Company, and it bore a facsimile signature of one Hiram J. Fairweather, President, who personally guaranteed payment. Hoke shoved the announcement into a locked drawer, along with the wallet. He sat for long hours, brooding over it.

Two weeks later, in a town called Oscuro where Dingus was believed to have previously committed certain felonies, several mail sacks containing federal papers were stolen from a post office. The postmaster who reported the theft also produced a crumpled piece of paper on which a scrawled note read *Dingus, the best time to steel them bags is after midnite.* A week after that, in another small town in the same area, certain ranch deeds and water titles were removed from a land office, and this time a kerchief was discovered on the scene, embroidered with the initials *DBM.* No cash money was involved in either larceny, according to the official circulars which subsequently crossed Hoke's desk, but each governmental department announced it was adding one thousand dollars to the over-all bounty nonetheless.

That still left Dingus five hundred dollars shy of the original ten thousand about which he and Hoke had spoken. "But he can go and manage the last of it hisself," Hoke decided, burying the mail sacks and sundry other evidence. "Meantimes this'll teach the critter to promise Hoke Birdsill a train and then not rob one, I reckon!"

But that had only been desperation. And anyway, it was over now. Now even the crowning public indignity of Turkey Doolan did not matter, especially since the loafers who had seen Hoke dragging the unconscious Dingus from Miss

Pfeffer's to the jail had quickly spread word of the new capture. (It had occurred essentially as Dingus himself suspected, of course. After escorting Miss Pfeffer to the doctor's, Hoke had lurked beneath her rear window for some moments first, to make certain that the snoring was authentic. What he'd hit Dingus with had not been a pistol, however, but a handy fry pan.) Hoke had explained the episode with modesty, if with a certain vagueness becoming characteristic in such situations, and then had arranged for his letter about the reward to depart with the morning stage. Now, still exultant, enthroned in his office he brushed the dust from a mail-order catalog, ready to consider the first possible additions to his wardrobe in the six long months since Dingus had been his prisoner before.

"Yep," he speculated aloud, "might even git me some Colts with gutta percha handles this time, like I seen that feller Bat Masterson wearing once, up to Dodge City."

Dingus merely snarled. Hoke had removed his handcuffs, but he continued to pace the cell like an abused animal, kicking at the spittoon one moment, at the slopbucket the next. The welt behind his ear was reddening also, which did not fail to compound Hoke's sense of gratification.

Much as he savored the moment, however, it occurred to him that he ought to look in briefly on Miss Pfeffer. "You reckon you won't start to weep for lonesomeness," he asked Dingus, "if'n I leave you in there by yourself fer a spell?"

"Go pee down a rattlesnake hole, you pistol-whipping mule-sniffer," Dingus told him.

"Poor old Dingus," Hoke chuckled. "You jest ain't got no sporting attitude, is all."

Nor could a confrontation with Miss Pfeffer's continued indisposition dampen his spirits either. When he had led her to the doctor's earlier she had been speechless, and in reply to questions about Dingus she had only wailed piteously; now, with the sound of Hoke's solicitous inquiry from her front door, she commenced to wail all over again.

The doctor was just emerging from her bedroom. "Sure does rend your heart, don't it, Doc?" Hoke commented.

"Rends something, I reckon," the doctor said ambiguously, whereupon Miss Pfeffer wailed anew.

"Hang it now, Agnes, it jest ain't all that tragic," the doctor called across his shoulder. "It's happened a couple times in history before, you know."

"Sure," Hoke contributed expansively, speaking toward the bedroom. "Lots of ladies has been terrorized by desperadoes. How about all them fair damsels got carried off by wicked dukes and such, as we had in school, only they was rescued by knights in shiny armour? Or in Mister Fenimore Cooper's writings, where—"

This time it was the doctor who seemed to moan, starting out.

"Well, say, you don't jest aim to leave her here alone?" Hoke asked (it had just come to him, if obliquely, that he did owe Miss Pfeffer a certain debt of gratitude).

"I got a sick team of oxen to look after, up to Denny Cross's place," the doctor said. "Man's got to make a serious living somewheres."

"But supposing she gets a relapse or something, after all the . . ." Hoke edged closer to the bedroom, peering within to see Miss Pfeffer gazing bleakly at nothing from beneath her blankets. "Why, a helpless woman all alone after a experience like that—I'd be right honored to sit a spell, ma'am, if'n you'd rest easier? I could jest blow out that lamp there, and then make myself to home in the parlor—?"

Hoke again thought he heard the doctor moan, or perhaps it was only the closing door. Miss Pfeffer sighed once. Then, distantly, with infinite weariness, she said, "Yes. Thank you. I—"

Then Miss Pfeffer did turn toward him, staring somewhat oddly in fact, as if she had only now become aware of his presence. But Hoke had already started to blow into the chimney. The light died.

"Well, now," he offered. Even in the new darkness he retained the impression that Miss Pfeffer continued to stare, though there was only silence. "I'll mosey on out front then, I reckon," he said finally.

"No. Wait. Mr. Birdsill, I—"

"Yes'm?"

Another moment passed. Miss Pfeffer's voice was strained. "Mr. Birdsill, I know it will sound forward of me, but—well, after that terrible encounter, thinking he was just a young man in difficulty, and then learning that he was . . ."

"The most murderous outlaw in the untamed West, yes'm. But you can relax now, because I done bested him in mortal combat and—"

"Yes," Miss Pfeffer cut in. "It was quite shocking. Mr. Birdsill, would you mind if—"

"What's that, Miss Pfeffer?"

"It's such a comfort to a girl to know that someone sympathetic is nearby. Would you remain here, Mr. Birdsill, in my room? On the chair? If you don't think it would be too compromising for an unmarried gentleman, I'd feel far more secure—"

"Well—why, sure, ma'am, I'd be more than—"

"Thank you, Mr. Birdsill. You're so understanding. You may use tobacco if you wish. As a matter of fact I'm partial to the odor."

"Well, it jest does happen I got me a cigar here," Hoke admitted.

He sat, smoking, holding his derby hat on his knee. They were quiet again. But still he had the sensation that Miss Pfeffer was considering him in that puzzling, thoughtful way.

Then Hoke suddenly believed he realized what it was. "Why, Miss Pfeffer," he cried, "you're truly ill from all you went through, ain't you?"

"Oh, it's nothing," Miss Pfeffer protested. "Nothing. Don't trouble yourself about poor me . . ."

"But I can hear you from all the way over here. You're—"

"No, I'm fine. It's only—"

"But ain't there something I can git you—more blankets or—"

"I'm afraid I'm using all of them already. Oh d-d-dear, it's—it's—"

"Well, we jest got to do *something,* or else you'll—"

"Oh, dear, if I only had a sister here, or some kinfolk. Because there's only one way to stop it. Oh, forgive me for even mentioning it, Mr. Birdsill, but—but—"

"Yes'm?"

"Oh, heavens, would you think me shameless if I—"

"Oh, ma'am, I couldn't think badly of a well-bred lady like yourself, no matter what."

"Well, it's—the only cure for a chill like this, is—oh, forgive me, but I'm certain you'll understand, in such emergency, if you c-c-could—"

"Miss Pfeffer! You want me to—?"

"It will be my death if you don't, I truly fear it will—"

"Oh," Hoke said. "Oh! You wait, then. I jest got to git out'n my—"

"Thank you, Mr. Birdsill. Oh, thank you. I feel warmer already, I truly do. But—dear heavens, this is so compromising, I hope you don't think—"

"Oh, no ma'am, I wouldn't never—"

"But—"

"Yes'm?"

"Isn't this the way people would—I mean married folk, of course—somewhat in this same manner, although with a certain arrangement, like—"

"Miss Pfeffer, *ma'am!*"

"And then like—"

"Miss Pfeffer!"

"Oh, dear," Miss Pfeffer said. "Oh, dear. And now the chill has come back, just dreadfully, dreadfully! Why, it's so bad, I don't believe I'll be able to stop shivering for anything at all—"

"Married?" Hoke cried. *"Married!* But—"

"Because I'm ruined, ruined!" Miss Pfeffer was weeping hysterically. "Oh dear, dear, how could you *do* this to me? A poor, defenseless girl like myself, trusting you, looking to you for protection in my moment of need—"

"But Miss Pfeffer, it weren't me who started the—"

"Oh, what have you *done!* Taking advantage of me when I

was helpless, helpless! You'll *have* to marry me. If you don't, I'll—"

"But Miss Pfeffer!" Hoke was fumbling for his trousers, swallowing hard. "But—"

"Stained, my honor stained forever! My virtue lost—"

"Please," Hoke pleaded, "Miss Pfeffer, get ahold of yourself. It weren't nothing more than—"

"I'll kill myself—"

"Huh?"

"If you don't make an honest woman out of me, I will! I must! There's no other salvation, none! And my blood will be on your hands, Mr. Birdsill!"

"But Miss Pfeffer, ma'am, I know I been courting you and such, but it weren't for—I mean I jest couldn't afford to go to Belle's too often, but now I already done got what I—I mean . . ."

Miss Pfeffer wailed in the darkness. "With a gun!" she cried. "I'll get a gun, and I'll put a bullet into my heart. Two bullets. Six! On your doorstep, Mr. Birdsill, for all the world to know who wronged me—"

"But I got to have some time, I . . ."

"Time?" Miss Pfeffer's voice changed abruptly, and again Hoke felt that she was eyeing him strangely. "How much time?" she asked him.

Hoke struggled with it. "A year?"

Miss Pfeffer wailed.

"A month, then?" Hoke ventured.

"Midnight," Miss Pfeffer declared.

"Midnight?"

"Midnight," she repeated. "It is now approximately ten o'clock. If you don't come to me with a man of the cloth by midnight, you will find my mortal remains upon the doorstep of the jail."

"A man of the—?" Hoke's head was swimming.

"Until then, Mr. Birdsill."

"But—"

He stumbled out, gathering his hat and coat mindlessly as he went. He was muttering to himself, all the way into the dark street, so he did not see the shotgun until it loomed beneath his very nose.

"Okay, you son-um-beetch," she said, "is no damn lie then, hey?"

"Huh?" Hoke had sprung back instinctively, his hands shooting up. He dropped his jacket. "Now blast it all, ain't I got enough troubles of my own without—"

But the enormous weapon was pressing against his chest now. "You make bim-bam with that horsy paleface, you son-um-beetch? Is true what I hear, hey?"

"Now who ever went and told you such a lie? And where'd you get holt of a shotgun like—"

"Never mind where I hear. Never mind shotgun neither. You try to get married up with that horsy twat or no, yes hey?"

"Aw now, Anna . . ."

"Stick up your damn hands again, you son-um-beetch."

"Now lissen here, I got things to do. There's a dangerous desperado over there in jail I got to keep track of. And on top of that I—"

"You keep track that one-arm feller instead, I think. I think you forget everything damn else, go find him pretty damn quick."

"One-armed feller? Find him for what? You mean that crazy preacher?"

"Preacher feller, oh yes, hey. I give you one hour, maybe two. Then damn quick you marry me, never mind that paleface bim-bam. I give you until midnight is damn all."

"*Midnight?*"

"Midnight," Anna Hot Water said. "Oh yes, hey. Otherwise I blow you apart from nuts to mustache, you son-um-beetch!"

She left him there, trailing her stench behind her.

He did not go back to the jail. In fact he would not have been able to say where he went at first, pacing the streets dismally. "And I can't even jest saddle up and skedaddle," he realized, "because I got to get Dingus hanged proper first, if'n I want to collect that new reward money."

He stopped at Belle's. Again he did not know why, except that the house itself, its sheer size, seemed to suggest sanctuary. In the main saloon he gulped several whiskeys, to no avail, however. He did not see Belle herself. People accosted him to ask about the new capture, but he scarcely heard what he told them. An image of Anna Hot Water's oiled flat head hovered before his eyes. When he squeezed them shut Miss Pfeffer's blunt, mare-like features replaced it. He saw himself surrounded by whimpering infants, all girls, all with mouse-colored, curl-papered hair.

So when he found that he had climbed to the door of Belle's office bedroom, standing indecisively but with a hand raised to knock, he still could not have said precisely what he had in mind. He had exchanged hardly a dozen words with Belle in six months. She took a moment to open, then appeared fastening a sleeveless robe about her waist. Muscles rippled in her blacksmith's arms, and she raised an eyebrow dubiously.

"Well," she told him, "so you're a big *hombre* again, are you? How much do you get that he can connive you out of this time—ten thousand almost, ain't it? What's on your alleged mind, Birdsill—you got some business, or do you think your new bank account makes us social equals who just ought to chat for a spell?"

But he wasn't really listening. So maybe it was the familiar bed behind her, the sheer enormity of that too, which had unconsciously drawn him. But the whole room itself, in the dim glow of a single lamp at the desk, intimated safety, security. Hoke knew the solution then. Because she could hide him here easily, certainly until his money arrived. "I'll pay you," he said. "I won't be too long, it's jest from Santa Fe. I'll give you five hundred dollars. And—"

"What?" Belle eyed him askance. "You'll give me—"

"Five," Hoke said. "All right, never mind. A thousand. But that's as high as I kin go. All I want is a few days, and . . ."

"Well, I'm damned," Belle said. "You mean to say—

because I've been offered twenty in my time, and once fifty, too, but that doesn't count since the varmint didn't have the cash to start with. But this is—"

"No," Hoke said. "You got the wrong idea, I jest mean—"

But Hoke did not get to explain. Because what suddenly happened then, what was already starting to happen even as he spoke, could not possibly have astonished or confused him more. Belle Nops abruptly swallowed once, then a second time, standing with one hand lifted to her immemorial bosom. Then the bosom heaved, and her face became contorted, and the swallowing became a series of ragged, inarticulate sobs. "A thousand dollars?" she choked. "A *thousand?*"

"Well, yair," Hoke said, "but I don't see no reason fer—"

And then Belle Nops was weeping. Tears flooded down her painted cheeks, beyond any control. "Oh, Birdsill," she cried, "you mean after six months you're that desperate? You truly missed me so much that—"

"*Huh?*"

"Never," she sobbed, "never! No man has *ever* cared that much before. And to think that I made you suffer so long, let your heart break for all this time!"

So now it was Hoke who had commenced to swallow, clutching his derby and stumbling backward against the door. "But—"

Moaning, her incredible bosom rising and falling, she lurched after him. Her eyes were wet, they gleamed. "A thousand dollars! In thirty-nine long years, never once have I been so deeply touched! Keep your money, keep it! I'm yours for nothing! Because I've missed you too! Oh, my sweetie, I've pined for you so!"

Hoke stumbled against a large stuffed chair, going over. "But I jest wanted to stay for—for—"

"Yes, stay—stay forever! We'll get married, now, tonight! Because it's so romantic I could . . ."

Hoke did not quite scream.

"Because I've always loved you," she cried. "From the very beginning!"

"But—but—all them names you used to call me, every time we—"

"Oh, you foolish, foolish boy, didn't you understand? It was because a girl can't be the one to say it, and you yourself were so blind, so blind! But what does the past matter now? What does anything matter? Oh, to think, at last—*Missus* Hoke Birdsill! Oh, my own sweetie pie—"

Flowing open, her robe enveloped him. The astonishing bosom unfurled like gonfalons loosed, like melons in dehiscence. But Hoke saw not, partook not. He had already fainted.

5

"We were drove to it, sir."

Cole Younger

At times like these, Dingus had to wonder where he had gone astray. "You old mule-sniffer," he asked himself thoughtfully, alone in the jail, "jest what is it, anyway, makes you so bad?"

But he believed he knew, really. "It's because I never had me a mother," he decided, "to guide me onto the correct paths of life."

For that matter he had never had a father either, or not for long, nor was his name actually Magee. He had been born William Dilinghaus but he had not been able to pronounce that, not when he was first old enough to understand that something else went with the Billy, and Dingus had been the result when he tried. Magee was a cousin. "You might as well call yourself whatever suits your liking," he had told the boy. "Because there ain't nothing else gonter come easy in this world, and that's the gospel."

On the other hand he did believe he remembered his father faintly, a short, pink-lidded man with hunched shoulders and gone prematurely to fat, and would dream of him from time to time. In the dream his father was ways sitting at a table, dealing cards. Then his head would jerk upright suddenly, as if worked by a bit between his jaws, and a small reddening hole would appear in the center of his forehead.

The cousin denied that Dingus could recall any such thing. "Because you was too young," he insisted. "Lissen, you weren't but two when I got the letter from that there peace officer and went rushing up the width of two states to claim you. So you jest must of heard me discoursing on the subject thereafter, is all."

What happened was this. His father had, in fact, been a gambler, although less than remarkably adept at his profession evidently, since the shooting Dingus thought he remembered, also an actual occurrence, had taken place after a particularly remunerative poker hand the man had won with three aces, two of which were unfortunately noticed to belong to the same suit. This was on a Mississippi steamboat, just north of Natchez. Deckhands were already in the process of weighting down the body, preparatory to depositing it over a rail, when the sound of a baby crying reminded someone that Dilinghaus had not come aboard alone. They found the boy in a lifeboat, teething on several additional mismatched high-denomination cards.

But there was no sign of any mother, on ship or when it docked either, nor did anything in the dead man's possessions allude to a wife. Indeed, the possessions themselves were few. Dilinghaus had left a cheap gold watch which bore an inscription (obviously a pun of sorts on his name, although of no help to the Natchez constabulary: *To my darling Ding, he rings the bell*) and a carpetbag containing unwashed laundry and more of the ill-served high cards. The local sheriff did find a letter in the bag, however, addressed to Dilinghaus in care of the steamboat line at Memphis, and wholly concerned with a debt of some thirty dollars owed by the deceased to one Floyd K. Magee of San Antonio. The sheriff wrote to Magee, explaining the situation and requesting any assistance and/or information the man might be able to provide.

Three weeks passed before Magee replied, admitting to an obscure relationship with Dilinghaus and authorizing them to send the child, after which the sheriff had to write a second time asking for the fare, and in the interim the boy was being kept in the local jail. But the jailer was a confirmed bachelor, and the sheriff had lost his own childless wife a decade before. They were practical men; after two days the pair of them had marched into the nearest brothel and picked the first whore in sight and arrested her.

She was relatively young, and she did not really seem to mind, but when three more weeks elapsed before Magee next told them to wait, that he would be there eventually in person, she finally said, "Look, it ain't living in a cell, and it ain't the kid neither, even though he does crap up his bottom faster'n I can keep count. But I've got six of my own up to Vicksburg, you understand? And there's my old drunk dad to support on top of that."

So they waited another day and then they solved that too, simply by moving the jailer himself into a cell and giving the woman the rear room in which he normally lived. (The room had a private entrance, and the neighboring madam cooperated by shunting certain of her clients through a back alley from the brothel. Meanwhile the woman had contrived a cradle by filling a drawer from the sheriff's desk with unginned cotton, and when necessary she simply replaced the drawer in the desk, removing the one above it for ventilation.) As a matter of fact they had become fixtures in the place, whore and orphan both, long before Magee finally did arrive. "It almost seems a shame," the woman commented at least once, "to go and hand him off to that cousin. A child needs a female's kind of tender looking after."

But the cousin felt differently. "I'm his blood kin," he said, "and I reckon I can do better for him than any prosty." "Yair," the sheriff said, "and you been right anxious to git around to it, seeing as how it were June when I wrote and now it's October." "I been busy," the cousin said.

He had been, and he continued to be, although five or six years would pass before Dingus understood at what. Where the cousin took him in San Antonio was an impoverished district not far from the ruins of the Alamo. The cousin was in his early thirties then, rheumy and myopic and of solitary habits (a neighboring half breed woman with some dozen youngsters of her own gave him advice or small aid with Dingus when needed). He never sent the boy to school, but he did take time to teach him to read out of an ancient anatomy text, and cope with the rudiments of arithmetic. It developed that the cousin had actually used the text in the study of medicine at one time, and certain of his acquaintants were practicing doctors in fact—several remote, secretive men who would knock on occasion, although never in daylight, and who never entered the shabby house either but would speak briefly and clandestinely with the cousin outside. That was when the cousin would be busy, those same nights. It would take almost until dawn.

And then one evening the cousin took him along. Dingus was eight then, and Magee did not explain. He said merely, "I reckon it's time you learned to make somewhat of a living." Dingus followed him for almost two hours along a road which crossed the length of the town before extending into the barren countryside beyond, gradually diminishing to become little more than tamped sand. Then they left the road to enter a once-cultivated but now abandoned field, and at a lightning-gutted hollow tree the cousin told him to wait while he boosted himself up and rooted around within the shell. When the cousin descended again he had two shovels with him, and a bulky folded canvas, apparently once part of the sleeve of a Conestoga wagon, but still he failed to elaborate. "Come on," was all he said.

But it was not much farther now, and Dingus had come to realize where they were anyway, had recognized the location if only out of recollected hearsay description and so began to comprehend vaguely some of the reasons for the furtiveness of their mission also, if not yet its specific purpose. When they entered the cemetery itself he began to get frightened. He said so. "Lissen," the cousin told him, "there ain't no physical thing on this earth a dead man can do, except wait for the worms to gnaw at him. So in a way we're doing him a kindness by preventing that. Get to digging, now. The dirt's easy enough, since it were jest put back this morning."

He was right about the latter part of it. They were finished in less than an hour, although the return trip consumed considerably more time than had the journey out. Dingus waited in an alley while the cousin delivered the improvised sack at the doctor's rear door. The cousin gave him a dollar, which he said was one third of what he himself was paid.

He went along regularly after that, perhaps once a week and doing more and more of the work as time passed (although he was restricted to digging only; he had always been small for his age, and even at ten could still barely lift, let alone carry). "But you can be grateful you're learning a trade," the cousin said, "especially since I been right upset, 'times, remembering what a unpromising start you had in life, and I weren't sure a unwedded feller like myself could bring you up Christian and respectable." "I appreciate it," Dingus said.

It was around then that it struck him to ask Magee about his mother also, but Magee could tell him nothing. "I never even heard tell your pa had got spliced," he said. "But you take a incompetent chap who slips a ace out'n his sleeve without he remembers it's the same ace of diamonds he's already got in his hand, I don't reckon he'll hold onto a wife any longer'n he's about to hold onto his money. Or his life. But anyways, I done my best to be a mother to you, likewise." "I appreciate that too," Dingus said.

But then the cousin died. It was rain, an unseasonal downpour which lasted two full nights and those ironically the first two in the cousin's life on which he had ever had consecutive employment. Dingus had caught a mild sniffle himself. Magee gave him nine dollars cash, and the engraved watch that had belonged to Dilinghaus, and the address of another cousin—a woman this time, in Galveston. "The nine dollars will get you there, I reckon," Magee said. "But what about burying you?" Dingus asked him. "Now lissen here," the cousin said, "what's the use of having a profession in this life if'n you can't calculate all the merits of it? There's a good one hundred graves out there with nothing but empty coffins in 'em, ain't there? And you're the sole individual after me knows the whereabouts of the most recent thirty or forty, ain't you?" "Oh," Dingus said, "sure now, I jest weren't myself fer a minute, is all." "Well, I forgive you," the cousin said, "since it's probably jest your grief over me has got you a little abstracted. I reckon a tyke would feel stricken at that, watching the demise of a cousin who give him everything he's got in this world." "I appreciate it all," Dingus told him.

That was about four o'clock on a Tuesday afternoon. The cousin died at sundown, and Dingus borrowed a neighbor's mule to remove him to the cemetery. He gave the matter considerable thought, finally committing the remains beneath the headstone of someone named McNutt, which seemed the closest he could come to Magee.

Then, when he was about to lead the mule homeward again, it stumbled into a freshly dug grave. Dingus could not get the animal out, nor was there much point in trying, since it had broken a foreleg. He brained it with his shovel. He told the neighbor about the mishap the next morning. "How much cash inheritance you got?" the neighbor asked.

"Nine dollars," Dingus said.

"Well, that were a useful mule, but it's the Christian thing, to take pity on a orphan newly sorrowing over his kin. Give me eight."

"It's gonter be right hard on me, getting to Galveston on only one dollar," Dingus said.

"Nonetheless it's proud experience for a boy," the neighbor insisted. "Like that Eastern feller Waldo Emerson is always saying, folks has got to learn self-reliance."

"Yes sir," Dingus said.

He debated selling the watch, and went so far as to ask a jeweler about it, but the jeweler told him it had never been worth very much to begin with. And the cousin had left nothing pawnable either, save perhaps for the old anatomy book. Dingus took that to one of the doctors.

"I really ought to keep it for a souvenir," he told the man, "since cousin Magee were so generous and kind in all the years, even to giving me one third of what we earned when all I done were the digging part. But I jest got to have some money."

But the book was out of date. "Why not wait a few days," the doctor suggested, "until the next time I hear about a burial, and then you could—"

"I still can't lift them," Dingus said, "being only eleven years old. I'd have to have a mule again, and then if I broke another leg I'd be in a real—"

"Borrow mine," the doctor insisted. "Yes, do. Because I'd hate to have it on my conscience that I hadn't assisted the nephew of a colleague. It can't be too long, and then you would have the full twenty dollars for—"

"How much?" Dingus said.

"Twenty dollars. What I always paid Magee. You're new at it, of course, but I'd be willing to pay the same amount that—"

"Oh," Dingus said. "Well, I appreciate that, I truly do. Where'd you say you kept that mule again?"

"Just out in back. But you can't simply go dig up any old thing, you know. The specimen has to be only recently interred, or—"

"I jest heard of one," Dingus said. "From yesterday evening, Tuesday, which ain't even twenty-four hours, and—"

"But who was—?"

"Feller named McNutt," Dingus said, already turning out. "I'll have him back here soon's it turns dark."

The next cousin was crazy, Dingus saw that immediately, although he could not have said precisely how. She was about forty, quite gray, and her skin was oddly colorless also, the hue of wet cardboard. She lived in an enormous old house, not her own, built in the Mexican style with linked, contiguous rooms facing an open inner courtyard, and before his arrival she had been completely alone.

But it wasn't that. Nor did he mind the prayers either, to which she woke him the first morning and which he learned he was expected to endure each evening as well, in dumb formal ritual not before any altar or image but in the unroofed garden itself, under the sky. "It is not God," the cousin said. "It is nature—the trees, the stars, the flowers—the all-embracing, transcendental oneness of things." "Yes'm," Dingus said. "Nor do I speak words when I kneel," she added. "I merely commune." "Yes'm," Dingus repeated.

So it took him a few days, and then he had to go to a keyhole to find out. It was wine. She had a bottle in her hand which she was just opening. When he went back to the door two hours later she was removing the cork from a second one.

Her name was Eustacia. He did not know what she lived on, and she complained repeatedly of poverty. "Moreover it costs a pretty penny to feed an extra mouth," she informed him, "although I do it gladly, out of a sense of the transcendental oneness of earth's creatures. I merely hope that you appreciate it." Frequently she had visitors, a group of anonymous and undifferentiated women of her own age and of an equal drabness who came singly or in clusters to sit for an hour. They were all unwed.

Like Magee, this cousin gave no thought to sending him to school either, although she finally did remark something she felt ought to be contributed to his up-bringing. This was just after he had gone to bed of an evening, perhaps at nine o'clock. He had not yet reached his fourteenth birthday. The cousin came into the doorway, considering him dubiously from beneath an upraised lamp. "I believe it is time you became cognizant of the facts of life," she said.

"What's them?" Dingus asked sleepily.

"Miss Grimshaw has volunteered to explain." Miss Grimshaw was one of the drab ladies, although Dingus could not have said which, even after the several years. Certain of them were teachers, and he expected her to appear with a book. But it was the cousin, Eustacia, who reappeared first, carrying a bottle of the wine instead. "Drink this," she told him.

"Drink it?" Dingus said.

"Drink it all," she insisted.

So when he awakened the next morning he still could not have said which one was Miss Grimshaw. "That's quite all right," the cousin said, "Miss Youngblood has volunteered to give you some further instruction tonight."

It went on for a year or so. More often than not it occupied six nights in each week also, since there were six of the drab ladies in all. "I hope you appreciate my efforts," the cousin said. "Above and beyond the financial difficulties, it is by no means easy for a maiden lady to bring up a young boy and be certain he is being educated as he should." "I'm most grateful," Dingus said.

And then this cousin died also. It happened suddenly, one Sunday morning. Or perhaps it had been Saturday night, since she was already stiff when Dingus found her. She lay sprawled before a chiffonier with her fingers locked about the neck of an unopened bottle of chablis. It took Dingus an hour or two to rid himself of his hangover (the drink had become as much a habit as the drab ladies by then), and then he made use of his earlier training to dispose of the body himself, in the overgrown courtyard. He even knelt briefly in the usual place, if a little uncertain about precisely to whom he was commending her pantheistic spirit. "Anyways," he said, "she put herself to considerable sacrifice on my behalf, and I hope she gets to be part of the transcendental oneness of things."

He found the address of a third cousin, someone named Redburn Horn, in one of her drawers, and, surprisingly, he also came upon some four hundred dollars in cash. The first stagecoach for Santa Fe, where Horn lived, was not due to leave Galveston until Tuesday morning.

So he was still in the house on Monday evening when Miss Grimshaw appeared. "Eustacia died," Dingus said.

"Oh," Miss Grimshaw said. "Oh, I'm dreadfully sorry."

"She were generous and kind."

"Yes, I'm sure. And now you're all alone."

"I'm gonter go to Santa Fe. I got one further cousin."

"Oh. But you're not leaving tonight, are you? I mean, since I'm already here, and it *is* my night, and—"

"Well," Dingus said, "I reckon if you made a special trip—"

She was gone in the morning, but he found the note on his table. *It didn't occur to me until I was ready to leave,* it said, *that I'd always settled with Eustacia herself, the poor dear. But I might as well pay you directly this time. The ten dollars is beneath the vase on the dresser. Sincerely, (Miss) Felicia Grimshaw.*

Cousin Redburn Horn turned out to be a poor substitute for a mother also, although this time the difficulty did not lie entirely with the man himself. He was a morose, disgruntled widower in his early forties who sold and repaired leather goods for a living, and did not always make that. He had been left with four daughters, the oldest of whom was a year younger than Dingus, and the family lived in three cluttered, disarrayed rooms behind Horn's shop. The man was arthritic, and he wore thick spectacles, and he talked idly about a dream of returning to the East. "Be hard to keep you," he told Dingus gloomily, "even if Christian charity demands it." Otherwise he rarely spoke at all, nor did he ask Dingus to help him in the shop (there was not enough work anyway). Dingus buried the four hundred dollars in an old sock, behind the woodpile.

So it was the oldest daughter, Drucilla. It took a while, because when Dingus reached Santa Fe she was scrawny yet, and anyway she ignored Dingus almost as completely as did Horn himself, either out of some ingrained familial shyness or perhaps simply because the dreariness which pervaded the household was contagious. In the beginning Dingus could not have cared less. He went his own way, and before he was fifteen he had taken to drifting into odd jobs at the nearby cattle ranches.

And then Dingus fell in love. He did not know how it happened, and on this particular occasion he had been away only four months, on a cattle drive to the Kansas railheads. But she had blossomed. Maybe it was her hair, which for the first two years had been severely braided but now hung unbound about her pink shoulders. Yet there seemed to be new flesh everywhere he looked also, and her breasts were suddenly indubitable. Within days Dingus was doing his utmost to lure her into the darkness of the leather shop after hours.

She finally hit him with an adze. "You stink of cow," she informed him.

"What's wrong with that? It's what I been riding behind the backsides of, is all."

He took a bath nonetheless, but that did not help either. "Because there just isn't anything romantic about you," she said.

He still did not understand, so she finally showed him the cuttings. She had a hatbox full of them, newspaper accounts and artists' sketches of General George Armstrong Custer, Captain W. J. Fetterman, Buffalo Bill Cody. "But that's loco," Dingus insisted. "All they done, they shot Injuns, and the true fact is, most of 'em got kilt theirselves in the process. Why, that Custer weren't nothing but a mule-sniffing, boastful, yeller-haired fool that dint have the sense to wait on the rest of his troops and got massacred for it, and anyways, you know darned well there ain't a hos-tile Injun within ten days of here no more. The few tame ones there is, they're jest on reservations. So how kin anybody go out and—?"

But Drucilla merely shrugged. So he had to do something. Because if it had been love before, within another month it was chronic desperation (worse, she bathed often, and he had discovered a peephole into the shed where they kept the tub). He owned a cow horse of his own, and a fourth-hand Remington revolver. When he saw her actually frame a portrait of Custer and then sigh wistfully as she nailed it above her bed, he saddled up and rode off.

The nearest reservation was two days away. He had about twenty dollars in his pocket, and he stopped the first dozen Indians he saw, asking where he might purchase old scalps. But most of them were Navajos and Pueblos who had never been belligerent to start with (some of the former tried to sell him blankets instead). One dispossessed old Zuñi finally told him the Spanish missionaries had long since confiscated all such distasteful trophies anyway.

So he had given up on it and was about to return home, disconsolately leaving the encampment by a different trail from the one he had followed coming in, when he noticed the Comanche wigwams. There were half a hundred of them, isolated and curiously forbidding, even somehow defiant in their withdrawal. Here and there an idle brave (they were all displaced from northern Texas) watched his passage with an expression openly truculent, and others looked up with similar unfriendliness from parched, unregenerate cornfields. It could have been his imagination, but Dingus hesitated to speak to any of them. Yet it struck him that love might find a way after all.

He waited in a secluded ravine until after dark, and then he slipped back on foot, making his way toward a wigwam before which he had seen a tall somber brave with a knife scar slashed the length of one cheek and the mark of an old bullet wound in his shoulder. "Because if'n the durned preachers done skipped confiscating souvenirs from any heathen in the territory," he told himself, "I'd bet me a whole cash dollar it's gonter be that gent right there."

The camp was silent, and a new moon was obscured by racing low clouds. Mongrel dogs prowled amid the wickiups but without barking, far too accustomed to abuse. There was no sound from within the selected wigwam itself.

Dingus knew that if any scalps were in fact to be found, they would be hanging decoratively from the tent's ridge-pole. With infinite caution, feeling ahead of himself, he crept within and toward it.

Then he stopped dead. His lifted hand had come to rest upon something quite warm, quite soft. It was more than human flesh, it was a portion of human anatomy that Dingus would not have needed cousin Magee's old textbook to recognize. He had been peeping at Drucilla's, daily. Before he could withdraw, sleepily, yet reponsively, even more than responsively, a voice muttered, "*Again*, White Eagle?"

Dingus kissed her. The question had been rhetorical anyway, a hand was already groping unmistakably. Hastily shedding his clothing, disguising his voice in a dull whisper, Dingus said, "Wait. Jest one second now, and I'll—"

So when she had at last commenced to snore peacefully again, while Dingus still struggled to collect himself, something else moved elsewhere in the wigwam. First Dingus heard a rustling of garments that were decidely not his own. Then the woman said, "*What?* Oh, now look, you raunchy old ramrod, how many times in one night do you think I—?"

Dingus had never reached the ridgepole. In fact he had lost his bearings completely, and now, fumbling anxiously in search of his pants, he stumbled into something standing behind him. He sprang away as it went over with a sound of crockery smashing. After that he was on his feet and sprinting.

But the brave was up also by then, and Dingus was unable to dodge the hand which snatched at him from behind; it took hold even as he plunged through the entrance. The moon emerged at that same instant. So they confronted one another for the moment as if frozen by the very flood of light itself, Dingus in his woolens with their rear flap commencing to tear where the brave gripped it, half turned away, and the brave himself even more starkly unclothed and with the nature of his interrupted indulgence even more stark than that. At first there was only puzzlement on the Indian's face. Then, still grasping the hatch of Dingus' drawers, but with the look turning to one of immemorial indignation now, like some great castrated beast the brave began to bellow. "A paleface! Not even one of those horny Mexican missionaries, but a paleface! In my own—"

But the flap finally gave. Already moving, as if his feet for that matter had not once ceased to move, Dingus plunged back within the tent and then scampered out again at its farther side, uprooting stakes and tearing wildly at skins as he wormed frantically through. The woman screamed, and the camp came alive as if under assault. Only the moon saved him, disappearing miraculously as quickly as it had appeared, while Dingus dove headlong behind stacked corn.

But no one was chasing him after all. Instead, the brave continued shouting where he stood, yet almost inarticulately for the moment so that the others seemed to be gathering about him more in curiosity than anything else, braves and women likewise, in their own assorted conditions of undress or interruption. And Dingus was still too much concerned with his own predicament to be startled at the fluency of the man's English either, once he became coherent again, especially since the brave was brandishing a gleaming Winchester rifle over his head now too. "That's it!" he cried. "That's it! The end, the absolute, fornicating end! Because they drove us from the hunting grounds of our ancestors, and we suffered that in silence! Because they gave us treaties from the Great White Father, and then they took our new lands as well, and we endured that likewise! Even when we've had nothing to eat but buffalo flop, we have accepted. But now an end! An end, I say! Because when they will not even let a man have his bim-bam in peace, I tell you it is time for *revenge!*"

He did not go back to Santa Fe immediately. As a matter of fact he stayed away for most of a week, knowing he would do so even as the Comanches mounted up and thundered from the reservation that same night, and so by the time he did return all of the dead had been safely buried, although certain of the larger buildings continued to smoulder. Cousin Redburn Horn himself had taken an arrow in the thigh, and although it was healing without complication the man was more anxious than ever now to return to the East. A cavalry patrol had long since been dispatched to hunt down the unpredictable renegades.

"And where were you?" Drucilla asked him. "Here when you finally might have had a chance to be a hero, you were off moping in the hills someplace."

"Well, it ain't my fault if'n I ain't lucky," Dingus said. "Anyways, looks to me like being a hero ain't no more than being in the wrong place at the right time, is all."

"Not that it matters to me one way or the other, actually," the girl said then, "since personally I couldn't care less about these banal Indian disturbances. It's really quite prosaic, you know."

"Huh?" Dingus said. "But what about all that there romance, and—"

"Oh, there's only one sort of truly romantic individual left in the contemporary West, obviously. I'm collecting different cuttings now."

She showed him a few. So this time it was even worse. "Jesse James?" he groaned. "Billy the Kid? But all they do, they rob things; is that what you mean? And for crying out loud, I heard a feller talking about Jesse one time, knowed him personal, and he told it for a true fact that he's got granulated eyelids. Now what in thunderation is romantic about a feller blinks all the time?"

"If you don't know, there's simply no help for you," Drucilla said with disdain, clipping a biography of the late James Butler Hickok from an old issue of *Harper's New Monthly Magazine*. Which left Dingus no less frustrated than before (the peephole had been filled in during his absence, also). Agonized, he scowled over her new collection until he knew many of the reports by heart. Finally he rode out again.

It took him months to muster the necessary courage. What he had in mind was a stagecoach waystation he had passed once, with a strong box too heavily padlocked not to hold something worth removing. He had to ride for some days, and his initial miscalculation should have been a sign. Because he planned to hole up in a mountain pass a short distance from the station and wait for dark, but when he reached the spot on a cloudless, sweltering midsummer day, it was well before noon. He was forced to perch on a flat rock for the necessary nine hours. When he unbent himself back into the saddle his horse took two sideward steps and fell dead.

"Not that it comes to much difference anyways," Dingus decided philosophically. "Because how is *Harper's New*

Magazine or anybody else gonter know what a notorious desperado you are less'n some writer feller happens to walk in and catch you at it?'"

The dilemma appeared insoluble. Nor had it altered on the afternoon months later when, quite by chance on a trail near Alamogordo, Dingus happened upon a stagecoach that had been attacked by unquestionably professional outlaws, and recently enough so that one injured horse still thrashed in the harness. Broken baggage was strewn about the road-way. The driving team and their four passengers lay face down in a gully, where they had been lined up and mur-dered. Dingus was horrified at the spectacle.

So he had just put the injured horse out of its misery, and was preparing to bury the victims, when something else caught his eye. Kicking at an embankment in its efforts to rise, the trapped animal had etched a deep, circular mark-ing with its hoof, very like the letter *D*. Dingus wet his lips, gazing at it.

There was no sound on the trail. Save for the vultures which hovered ominously above, there was no movement either. A small, sharply pointed twig actually lay at his feet, as if in conspiracy. Dingus was holding his breath. Then, snatching up the twig at last, and with furtive, darting glances about himself, hurriedly but clearly he left his portentous message in the dust: *Dingus Billy Magee done this. Beware.*

Two weeks after that, in a town called Pendejo where he himself was a total stranger, he overheard gossip about another crime altogether, as yet unsolved. But by then he had been waiting with gleeful impatience to stumble upon just such a situation. The Pendejo sheriff had been shot in the back. "When'd it happen?" Dingus asked casually. "Jest last night sometime," a waiter told him. Dingus himself had reached the town not an hour before. He nodded sagely. "Might have figured," he said, "since I passed Dingus Billy Magee on the trail out of here this morning."

"Dingus whoozy what?"

"Well now, you fellers jest must be behind the times up here, I reckon," he informed them blandly. "Why, if'n there's a more disreputable, underhanded, back-shootin', poorhouse-robbin' skunk in the whole New Mex territory, it'd be news to most folks. Yep. What I hear, this Dingus Billy Magee, he cuts the gizzard out'n law officers on sight sometimes, jest from plain cantankerousness. That's Dingus, D-I-N-G-U-S—"

So it took scarcely any time at all after that, and when he started back to Santa Fe again, perhaps three months later, there was already well over two thousand dollars in rewards on his head, and his name was being spelled reasonably also. "Which even Juicy Drucy is gonter have to admit ain't bad a-tall, for a shaver not even yet nineteen," he speculated satisfactorily. He had taken to offering physical descriptions of himself on recent occasions also, inventing the red-and-yellow fringed Mexican vest by way of embellishment, and that too had been mentioned in several accounts of his exploits. Shortly before he reached home it occurred to him that he might actually purchase one.

So Drucilla had never heard of it, of the famous garment or of any of the rest, apparently. "Because I never read the newspapers any longer," she said contemptuously. "Why, no respectable girl would have any interest in violence and bloodshed, which is all they ever print these days, of course."

Dingus gaped at her. "But all them cuttings you—"

"When one ceases to be a child, one puts aside childish things. I should like to marry a pillar of the community now, a banker perhaps. Yes, indeed, nothing but a banker will do."

"A *what?* Well, I'll be mule-sniffing son of a—"

"Cousin William, please. Your language!"

So he endured that for a week or two and then he asked her how much it would cost to buy a bank, or open one. "Oh, I imagine it might be managed for sixty or eighty thousand dollars," she informed him, "since I would only be interested in a respectable sort of bank, naturally." "Sixty or eighty *thousand!*" Dingus screamed. "Lissen, I got four *hundred,* in a sock I buried one time, and that's the—"

And then suddenly it came to him. She was in the kitchen, sweeping, and he literally dragged her into the yard. "All right," he said. "Yes. But wait now. Jest wait, a month or so maybe, because it ain't gonter be that easy. But there's got to be the sixty, maybe even more. Because it's been ten years, at least, that she's been salting it away, and—"

"Who?" Drucilla said. "What are you—?"

It was Belle Nops. Dingus did not know her except casually, since he had stopped at the bordello only rarely in his wanderings as a trailhand. But he had heard the speculation among her more regular clients often enough, and now his mind began to glow with the possibilities. "Because at a dollar a hump for all them years it's got to be a unadulterated fortune," he said. "And on top of that there's the profits from the drinking and the gambling likewise. And it's all jest sitting there, in that safe which fellers says is in her office, and which—"

"But I still don't know what you're—"

"You jest start cogitating on exactly where you want that bank to be," Dingus said, "and I'll be back here in less'n a month." He did not explain further, already leading his horse from the barn. "Oh, yes, indeedy," he told himself, saddling up. "And it's been getting on time I went and done me some *honest* stealing, anyways."

But it wasn't a month. Nor was it two or even three. He tried flattery first, but this did not even get him into the bedroom, the office. "Because you lissen here now, Sonny," Belle Nops told him, "I nominate my own jockeys, and I ain't so saddle-wore that they're about to be snotty twerps wet behind the ears yet, neither. Anyways you'd rattle around like a small dipper in a big bucket." "But I knowed me a right smart of older ladies," Dingus protested, "and they'd speak admiringly of me, too. Why, you jest write a brief letter of inquiry to Miss Felicia Grimshaw, over to Galveston, say, or Miss Youngblood in the same—" "I just this morning hired on a unplucked little thirteen-year-old from Nogales," Belle told him, "down the hall in the end room. Three dollars cash money, you can do the first-night honors."

So then he stole a key and tried rape. What he had in mind, of course, was an eventual intimacy that would lead to his presence on an occasion when the safe was opened. But he had never been exceptionally strong, nor did he weigh as much as a hundred and forty pounds, and she outwrestled him easily each time. He had been jumping her from behind the door. When he changed his tactics and did not material-ize from within her closet until she stood stripped to her gar-ters, she finally got mad enough to heave him bodily down the rear staircase.

Dingus sprained a wrist. But if he had to give up on it for a time after that, he finally did commit one actual crime while nursing the injury in a sling. He was not sure how much educational value the experience offered, the victim being an acquaintance. Too, he had intended appropriating the man's derby hat only; the slightly moist eight hundred dollars from within it was sheer happenstance.

When a new strategy at last did occur to him, it was based on the theory that recumbency would be half the battle. So this time he waited outside the bordello entirely until he believed she would be asleep. Then he made use of his key, undressed soundlessly, and slipped into her elusive embrace.

Some weeks after that, when he was two days away from being hanged, he complained moderately to Hoke Bird-sill. "Least you might have done," he said, "you could of wore that there new sheriff's star on your woolens, I reckon, so a feller'd know jest who it were he was about ready to violate."

But even after he had talked Hoke into letting him escape, simultaneously appropriating the latter's reward money as an afterthought, the sense of his unfulfilled mission continued to plague him. It had become a matter of more than Drucilla and their bank; there was a man's pride. Yet in his next two attempts he did not even reach the bordello itself, what with Hoke lying in wait for him behind it.

Dingus supposed he could not blame Hoke for a certain annoyance, though as a matter of truth the man's intrepidity puzzled him. "Maybe I oughter of added it where Johnny

Ringo and the Dalton brothers involved with Mister Earp in the valiant story of how I got my wrist wounded that time," he speculated. When Hoke put a bullet through the loaned-out vest for the second consecutive time, Dingus concluded the project could wait again after all. He decided he might as well add Hoke's three thousand eight hundred dollars to the four hundred in his sock at Santa Fe.

But he was still some distance away, curled foetally into his blankets on a chilly night west of the Pecos, when he had a new educational experience altogether. He had no opportunity to flee as the two men appeared, since they materialized so unexpectedly in the flickering glow of his campfire, and so soundlessly, that for an instant he almost believed it a dream. In fact the first thing he saw was the naked bore of the sawed-off shotgun itself, as it was thrust beneath his chin. "One move and you're deceased," he was told.

But then he was less afraid of being murdered intentionally than of having it occur by accident, since the man covering him was so nervous that the shotgun commenced to tremble unconscionably in his hands, pointing into Dingus' left eye one instant, his navel the next. Nor was the second thief any more composed. Snatching up Dingus' weapons, he dropped each of them at least once before managing to scatter them beyond reach in the mesquite.

Then, abruptly, constellations exploded inside Dingus' skull. So the conversation which followed seemed dream-like also:

"Great gawd amighty, what did you clobber him for?"

"Well, will you jest look! All that there cash! I thought he'd be jest some cowpuncher on the trail, prob'ly, but this critter is very doubtless a outlaw hisself, I mean a authentic one, and—"

"Well, it's too late now, since we got it half took anyways."

"Oh, I jest knew it! I jest knew we'd git our fannies stomped on. Because now he's likely to hunt us down fer revenge, or—"

"Well, we still got to take it. Because we been intending at least one gen-u-ine daring deed fer years now, instead of jest

*writing to them newspapers, and this has got to be it. I'll get
the horses."*

*"Shouldn't we oughter bind him up, maybe? I mean it, I'm
right scared, Doc—"*

"Let's jest get the b'Jesus out of here fast, Wyatt—"

Then he had one further lesson to muse upon when
he reached Santa Fe itself, since Horn's leather shop was
already boarded up when he got there, and cousin Redburn
and his three younger daughters were in the very process
of loading a wagon with what appeared to be the totality of
their household effects. Nor was Drucilla herself anywhere
in evidence. Cousin Redburn glanced at Dingus as if he had
been absent no longer than a matter of days. "Come into
a bit of cash currency," he announced matter-of-factly, "so
I'm heading back East like I always wanted. Real windfall it
were, I do admit."

"What?" Dingus said. "Cash? Lissen, you didn't happen
to go and find no four hundred dollars in a old sock out back
in the—?"

"Well say, ain't it a coincidence that I done jest that! But
how on earth would you happen to of guessed it, Dingus?"

"How? Only because it's my own durned last-remaining
money, is all. How else do you think, you mule-sniffing
old—"

"I don't reckon you could prove that, could you, nephew?
A notorious outlaw like you turned out to be? Now who do
you think would accept your word against that of a respectable, hard-working shopkeeper who done took you in one
time out'n Christian decency, and you jest a poor waif of an
orphan then too?"

Dingus did not argue. He didn't cave, even after what he
had already lost. "All right," he said, "never mind that. At
least this time it's straight stealing again anyways, upright
reaching in and taking it, which puts you in a class with some
better folks than the rest of my cousins. It's almost a pleasure.
But where's Drucilla? That's what I come back for anyways,
not no piddling four hundred dollars or—"

"Ain't heard, huh?" cousin Redburn asked.

"Heard what?"

"Well now, old Drucy, she done got married up with a lawyer feller."

"She done *what?* With a *who?*"

"Yep. Right interesting story, too. You recollect that Comanche uprising here in town, back a while ago? Well, seems like what started it, it were some white feller diddling around with Comanche pussy, although as a matter of fact nobody could ever rightly learn that part of it too straight. But anyhow there was this one big buck was involved someway, and it seems he jest never did get over bearing a grudge. So even after the territorial governor declared a amnesty, this particular critter, he kept agitating troubles. Big foul-looking monstrosity, got a knife scar down one side of his face, and been shot in the shoulder once, likewise. And the ironic part was, he weren't even married, but it appears what annoyed him was a white man carnal-ing jest any squaw a-tall. So anyways it turns out, he broods and broods back there on the reservation all this time, and then one day he comes riding on into town here, right smack down the main street bold as a fart in church. Couple of fellers like to shot him on sight, nacherly, but what with that there amnesty and all, well, they think twice about it. So meanwhile this here buck, by now he's over to the main plaza, out front of the Fred Harvey Hotel it were, and the next thing you know, he's sitting there crosslegged on the ground with his horse hobbled under a tree. Jest asittin', is all, like maybe he's resting a spell. He had a supply of jerkey with him, I reckon, or whatever all else it is them heathens eat, because the next thing after that, darned if'n he didn't keep right on sitting there too, fer four whole days and nights. Weren't nobody could figure out what he had in mind neither, except for watching folks contemptuous-like, and he sure done a heap of that, staring beady-eyed at anybody who went on by. Got to be a mite spooky after a time, sure enough, and some of the folks with shops down that way didn't appreciate it nohow, since a right smart of the wives in town had already took to doing their purchasing elsewhere. So it's likely he would of got shot after all, if'n he didn't finally quit it. And by then we should of had some notion what he planned on doing, of course, seeing as how he hadn't done it that anybody'd noticed before that, not once in the four days or nights. It must of been jest before dawn when he skedaddled, although nobody seen him go, but then the next morning it was like he was still sitting there anyhow, in a way, since folks had got so used to taking a nervous glance at him there still weren't nobody could pass the spot without they looked over now also. Which must of been jest what he calculated on, in his scornful manner, because right there it stood, heaped up fer all to see and looking like there weren't no human being in this world, and not even no redskinned one neither, could leave that much of a monument behind with jest one solitary dumping of his bowels—"

"Well hang it all," Dingus demanded, "what do I care about that? What has that got to do with—"

"Well, I'm getting there, if'n you'll be patient," Redburn Horn declared. "Because it weren't no more'n half a week later, and darned if'n he weren't back again. This whole affair itself weren't no more'n eight, ten days ago, incidentally. So anyhow this time the sheriff gets holt of him right quick, but now the Injun promises he won't commit no more public nuisances. Because anyways he don't intend to be here long enough for that, not this visit. Because this time what's he do but parade right on into the courthouse and ask for a paper to be notarized. And not only is the paper writ in English, and by his own hand, but darned if'n he don't talk the language better'n most native-born white folks, too. And what's the paper, meantimes, but a draft on some Boston bank for *five thousand dollars,* cash currency of the United States of America, and which the judge verifies for him likewise, and which he then takes on over to Zeke Burger's clothing emporium and commences to buy clothes with. And not jest regular duds neither, like the usual calico shirt a ordinary Injun'd buy, but the absolutely fanciest stuff Zeke's got in stock—like striped pants and what do you call them things, frock coats, and a gen-u-ine silk top hat to boot. And by this time there's half the loafers in town looking through the window, of course, and after that when he walks on over to the stage office and asks for a ticket for as far north as you got to travel to catch a railroad train to Massachusetts, well now there's not only the remaining half of the loafers but a good smart of the working folk in addition. And after this when it develops there ain't no transportation until tomorrow, darned if'n the next thing he don't do is march across to the hotel and request a place to sleep—and not jest no plain bedroom neither, mind you, even though the last time the polecat was in town he'd reposed under a cottonwood tree fer four consecutive nights, but he wants a whole durned sweet. Now old Phineas Austin back of the desk, he ain't about to rent out no room or no sweet neither, not to no redskin, even if'n the redskin does happen to be outfitted like some Egyptian duke or something, but then the judge tells Phineas he better go ahead or else the Injun is apt to purchase the whole danged hotel and fire him. Because what happened is this. He were a full-blooded Comanche all right, but it seems when he was maybe nine years old he got lost one time, and hurt too, and some white folks in a passing stagecoach got holt of him—not only jest took care of him fer a spell, but finally even brung him all the way East and give him a education. Name's White Eagle in Comanche, but it's also Sidney Lowell Cabot Astor or some approximate thing in American, all plumb legal from where them Easterners eventually adopted him to boot. Evidently he'd got restless after a spell, and had come back on out this-a-way, but now all of a sudden his foster father had caught the dropsy and died. Letter must of got to the reservation while he were in town here perpetrating that turdheap the week before, I reckon, but anyways he'd done inherited something akin to ten full street-blocks of downtown Boston, if not to mention a whole fleet of ocean-traveling boats, and some railroads, and the biggest law company in the state of Massachusetts. I forgot to mention that part, that he'd got educated in the law hisself. And that was when it came to pass with Drucilla, you see, when the judge happened to remark about that. Because I reckon you been away too long to know, but that Drucilla, why she jest had her heart set on marrying up with a lawyer feller, fer, oh, at least two or three months now, Dingus—"

That was something less than half a year ago. At first Dingus had been more confused than dismayed, but the confusion had stemmed from just the fact that there was no dismay. So it took him only a few days to realize that he had actually ceased to think about Drucilla a good while before. All he really cared about was that safe.

Nor was it the money either, the sixty or eighty thousand dollars which might surprise him by being considerably more than that. It was principle. Yet he did not rush back to it, on the premise that man cannot rush destiny anyway. Instead, he dropped hints and promoted rumors until some four thousand five hundred dollars in new rewards had accrued to his name. And even then he thought of this as mere exercise, as a sort of renewed apprenticeship before the ultimate, irreproachably professional enterprise of the safe itself.

But it amused him to wait, also, since it further enhanced the mood of anticipation. Deliberately he set out on a long, aimless journey into Old Mexico, where he had never been, to prolong it.

So then in Chihuahua he caught dysentery, a case so extreme that it not only postponed his return to Yerkey's Hole for some months, but precluded mobility of any sort in the interim. "Less'n I want to leave a trail clear across the territory that even a old stuff-nosed mule-sniffer like Hoke Birdsill couldn't miss," he said.

Then, when he did return to New Mexico, the first thing he discovered was that the bounty on his head had mysteriously more than doubled, in major part because of a posting by something called the Fairweather Transportation Company, of which Dingus could have sworn he'd never heard. "But maybe I ought to get to it at that," he decided, "if'n they even made it a criminal offense when I shit now." He was some two weeks' distance from Yerkey's Hole when he picked up an innocuously moronic drifter named Turkey Doolan and headed west.

He had no attack in mind, only an abiding, bemused sense of confidence, as if the entire project were now less a matter of premeditation than of ordination, of fate itself. And even when Hoke Birdsill turned out to be as irascible as ever, not only banging Turkey Doolan from the saddle but wounding Dingus himself, Dingus remained merrily undaunted.

So he was still laughing, still delighted with the world he had merely put off conquering until tomorrow, when he took time out to deceive a drab, horse-faced woman named Agnes Pfeffer.

"Well, anyways," he rationalized some few hours later, "at least it were a nostalgic sort of error, since I'm darned if'n she dint remind me jest a trifle of both Miss Grimshaw and Miss Youngblood theirselves."

So it wasn't Hoke Birdsill he was angry with tonight when he awoke in the bleak, familiar cell, of course, it was his own irresponsibility. Because he actually believed the conclusion he was to reach once Hoke left him alone to brood over his new incarceration. "That's it, sure as outhouses draw flies," he declared in resignation, fingering the swelling lump behind his ear. "A feller has to face life without a mother to guide him, he's jest nacherly doomed to tickle the wrong titty, 'times."

Nor would there be any solution quite so simple as talking his way into a fake escape this time, Dingus knew. In fact Hoke seemed determined to give him no opportunity to talk about anything at all, since it had been well before ten o'clock when he departed, voicing his intention to look in on the indisposed Miss Pfeffer, and now at eleven there was still no sign of him. Although perhaps it was not quite eleven at that, since Dingus still made use of the old, engraved watch of his father's which cousin Magee had given him, and it had long ago ceased to be reliable. "But jest the fact that I keep it proves I'm downright sentimental at heart," he mused, "which shows all the more how I would of surely paid dutiful heed to a mother's advice."

Meanwhile the confinement had already begun to annoy him physically, albeit mainly because he was still unable to sit. He had dressed himself, once Hoke had removed the handcuffs, but he had been pacing restlessly ever since. On top of which it hurt where Hoke had bushwhacked him in Miss Pfeffer's bed.

So he was still pacing when the woman, the squaw he had met earlier, came striding suddenly into the empty main room of the jail. And for a moment, preoccupied, Dingus did not even recognize her. Then he literally bounded toward the bars. Because she was still carrying his shotgun.

"Hey!" he cried, glancing to the door to make certain she was alone at the same time. "Howdy there! Remember me? From that there gun, when—"

But she ignored his interests completely, scowling in a preoccupation of her own. "Where that loose-button son-um-beetch?" she asked. "I decide never damn mind midnight, he marry up with me right now I think, hey?"

Dingus could scarcely recall what she was talking about, if he even fully knew. "Yeah, sure, anything you say," he told her anxiously. "But lissen, that gun—it's mine, remember? From out by that wagon, I give it to you. But it were only a loan, you understand? And now I need—"

She finally paused to consider him. "Oh, is you, hey? How you feel now, you still in bum shape? How come you in there anyways, yes?"

"Howdy, howdy, yair, I feel jest fine," Dingus dismissed it, "but never mind that now, let's—" She was holding the weapon inattentively, one finger through its trigger guard, and Dingus strained as if attempting to will her toward him. "Come on, now," he pleaded. "I jest couldn't carry it before, being hurt and such, but now I need it urgent again. Look, you got to—"

So then she was paying him no regard at all once more, clomping across to glance briefly into the back room, and then considering the desk. "He don't come back here yet, hey? Not since I see him up there, suck round that pale-rump teacher-lady place?"

"Oh, look, look, I don't know nothing about that—"

Dingus' voice was rising, becoming mildly hysterical. "Ma'am—Miss Hot Water, ain't that it?—look, please now, you jest got to give me that gun back. And before nobody else comes along neither, or it'll be too—say, here, look, I'll even buy it from you, I'll give you . . ." He was fumbling anxiously in his pockets, then desperately. He had been carrying several silver dollars when he had undressed at Miss Pfeffer's. His pockets were empty. "Oh, that unscrupulous, self-abusing old goat, even thieving from a unconscious prisoner, I'll—aw, lady, please now, give me the—"

"You a pretty young feller be in hoosegow. What your names anyway, hey?"

"Dingus," he sobbed absurdly. "Look, lady—ma'am—I jest got to have my—"

But Anna Hot Water was suddenly frowning, tilting her rhombic blunt head. "Din-gus?" she said. She mouthed it slowly, in part with its common pronunciation but with over-tones of the way it was enunciated by Indians or Mexicans. Then she said it again, wholly now in the second manner. *"Dean Goose?"*

Then something began to happen to Anna Hot Water. Her mouth was slack, and her eyes turned cloudy. For a long moment, while Dingus agonized over the shotgun, one arm actually stretching helplessly through the bars toward it now, stroking air, she seemed to be in agony herself, in an ordeal of what might have been attempted thought. Then he saw her begin to grasp it, whatever it was. Her eyes widened and widened.

"Dean Goose?" she repeated tentatively. "Feller stop one time up to Injun camp near Fronteras? Feller take on seventeen squaws in twenty hours nonstop and squish the belly-button out'n every damn one? Dean Goose? You *that* Dean Goose feller?"

"Well, yair now," Dingus stated, "I reckon I been through Fronteras, but what's—"

But he did not get to finish, because the rest of it happened so quickly then, and was so inexplicable, that for an instant he was totally at a loss. In fact for the first fraction of the instant he was terrified also, since he thought the shotgun was being aimed at himself. So he was actually leaping aside, sucking in what he believed might well be his last breath, when the gun roared, although by the time she had cast it away and flung the smashed cell door inward he had already realized, had understood that her aim had been true if still comprehending little else. Her face was radiant. She tore at her clothes.

"Dean Goose!" she cried. "Dean Goose for real, greatest bim-bam there is! Never mind that floppy-dong old Hoke Birdsill, oh you betcha! Come to Anna Hot Water, oh my Dean Goose lover!"

He felt his bandage tear loose as he vaulted Hoke's desk. He had to sprint the width of the town before he was certain he had lost her.

He broke stride once, dodging behind Miss Pfeffer's house to snatch up a fistful of the revolvers he had deposited there earlier, but she was still close enough behind him at that juncture that he had to leave his holster belts in the entangled sage, along with his Winchester. He ran on with the Colts clattering inside his shirt.

When he had finally drawn clear, he found that he had stopped not far from the dilapidated miners' shacks he had seen before. In fact the lamp still burned in the one where he had come upon Brother Rowbottom, the dubious preacher. It took him time to catch his breath, especially since consideration of the manner of his deliverance had set him to laughing again, but eventually he limped back over there.

The man himself still sat amid the disheveled shacks as if having scarcely moved in the several hours except perhaps to raise the whiskey jug, which was wedged between his bony knees at the moment. He wore the same disreputable woolens, and the light reflected dimly from his hairless lumpy skull. His empty left sleeve had become wound around his neck, draped there.

He did not appear thoroughly drunk, however, and he eyed Dingus quizzically. "So you come on back, eh? Heard the call of the Lord's need after all, did you?"

"I were jest passing the vicinity," Dingus replied. "If'n you'll excuse the intrusion, I'll make use out'n your lamp." Not waiting for an answer (none was forthcoming anyway) Dingus set aside his weapons and then lowered his pants, twisting about to inspect the dressing. He had bled again, but not significantly. Watching him, or perhaps not, the man, Rowbottom, belched expressively.

"I reckon you'd better give me that damn dollar," he decided then, as Dingus readjusted the bandage. "The Lord don't cotton to critters repudiating His wants two times in the same night."

But Dingus was not really listening. Because if he could afford to be safely amused again, it also struck him as time to turn serious about certain matters. "I reckon I'd best at that," he told himself, "afore I wind up too pooped out for even simple stealing." He fastened his belt, wondering if Hoke Birdsill had heard the shotgun.

"So do I get the lousy dollar or don't I?" the preacher wanted to know.

Dingus reached absently into a pocket, then into a second one before recalling that Hoke had emptied them. But at the same time the first remote intimation of an idea was crossing his mind. He lifted his face to meet Rowbottom's flat, oddly refractive eyes.

"You shy of cash money pretty bad, are you?" he asked then.

"The Lord's work ain't never terminated," the man said.

"Tell you the truth now, I weren't rightly thinking about His'n," Dingus said, still pensive. "You got any sort of scheme in your head, maybe, about how a feller might go about getting a certain local business establishment empty of folks fer a brief spell? Like say a certain whorehouse—if'n you'll pardon the term?"

"Womenflesh runs arampant," the man shrugged. "I been trying my best. But you drive 'em out one door, they jest hies their abominations back through the nearest winder."

But now Dingus was attending more to the tone of the man's voice, its resonance, than to the content of his speech. "I dint mean preaching," he explained. "You reckon folks'd hear you from a fair piece, if'n you had a sort of public announcement to make—say a announcement worth maybe twenty cash dollars?"

The preacher had been raising the jug. He dropped it as if struck. "Brother, leave us not bandy words. For twenty dollars cash currency I would hang by my only thumb at Calvary itself, hind side to."

"Never mind getting no horse soldiers involved," Dingus said. He retrieved the oldest of his Colts, hefting it momentarily. Then he tossed it pointedly onto the shuck mattress.

So then the preacher sat absolutely without movement, staring at the weapon, for perhaps ten seconds. "*Fifty* dollars," he proclaimed finally. "The Lord couldn't condone mayhem for less."

"Ain't mayhem neither," Dingus said. "That there's your pay. Twenty-*two* dollars, more like, standard saloon pawning price on the model."

So the preacher inspected it then, trying the hammer gingerly several times. Then it disappeared all but miraculously beneath the shucks, as the man himself arose and stepped decisively toward the peg from which his clothes were hung. "The Lord's will be done," he intoned.

Dingus considered his antiquated watch as the man dressed. It was approximately eleven-thirty.

"Starting in jest about fifteen minutes from now," he said, "all up and down the main street, but most especially up to Belle's. Loud as you kin call it out, I want you to inform folks that Dingus Billy Magee done escaped jail again. And that he's putting it to Hoke Birdsill to meet him fer a pistol shoot." Dingus thought a moment. "Yair. Pronounce it fer out front of the jailhouse, at midnight sharp."

Brother Rowbottom could not have been more

unimpressed. "Feller name of Dingus Freddie Magee has got escaped again," he repeated without emphasis, "and he hereby challenges Hoke Birdbelly to a fight with hoglegs, front of the jail come midnight. That the entirety of it?"

Dingus nodded, still contemplative. "But you pronounce it jest afore twelve up to Belle's, that's the crucial part. Folks'd be more interested in the chance they could see a bloody murder, than in jest some common everyday one-dollar poontang, don't you reckon?"

"Ain't mine to judge," the preacher said. "The Lord sends me His missions in devious ways. You plumb sure I kin get twenty-two dollars on that Peacemaker single-action? Firing pin's a mite wore, there."

"You don't," Dingus said, "and somewhat later'n midnight I'll give you payment for it myself—in dust gold or minted silver or paper currency or any other form you so desire."

The preacher eyed him opaquely, buttoning a threadbare frock coat. Then he belched again.

"Amen," Dingus said.

"So you're a lamb of the Lord after all, eh?"

"Jest insofar as nature is concerned," Dingus said. "Trees and clouds and such, sort of transcendental."

So this time the preacher broke wind. "Emersonian horse pee," he grunted.

But Dingus had already closed his eyes, leaning against the wall until he heard the man depart. Then, fingering the most recent bullet hole in his trustworthy vest, and with his young brow furrowed from the gravity of it all, he commenced to devise the remainder of his strategy.

"So even if'n I never had no mother at that," he remarked aloud, "ain't nobody gonter be able to say Dingus Billy Magee dint truly apply his talents in this life, after all."

But certain sensuous remnants of the preacher's flatulence were abruptly wafted toward him then, and he had to go hurriedly elsewhere.

6

---

*"A loaded man is hopeless
against a loaded six-shooter."*

Walter Noble Burns

Turkey Doolan was to see most of it. Nor would he ever forget.

At first, in the dim cast of light from a lamp in an adjacent room, he did not remember where he was. Then, when he recognized the doctor's office, when he found himself shirtless and with a fresh neat swath of bandage below his left armpit, he endured a moment of acute anxiety. He sat up gingerly, exploring flesh with his fingertips. But there was little pain, even when he pressed forcefully against the gauze itself. So then a new expression came into his freckled face. It was a look of unrestrained enchantment. "Boys," Turkey said, and almost aloud, "yes sir, I dint jest *know* Dingus Billy Magee, but him and me was such fond chums—why one time over to the New Mex, darned if'n that Hoke Birdsill dint go and near assassinate me fer Dingus by mistake!"

Breathing deeply, deliciously, Turkey stood. Then he paused again, gazing at his boots where they lay beneath a chair, at his shirt folded on the seat. "Doc?" he said tentatively.

The vest was nowhere to be seen. Turkey's eyes darted about the small, sparsely furnished quarters. "Now where the hang—?"

So when he heard the sound again, not realizing that this was what had awakened him to start with, he paid no attention, or not immediately. Then, thunder struck, he bolted to the window.

"Escaped?" he muttered. "And done challenged Hoke Birdsill to a—?"

Turkey could barely discern the shouting man himself in the outer darkness, other than to judge him to be tall and evidently bald. He was already some distance away, moving in the direction of Belle Nops' bordello, although his voice was remarkably sonorous. "Dingus got escaped again?" Turkey repeated. *"Again?"*

But it wasn't that, wasn't the puzzlement that mattered. It was the remainder of the announcement, as its overwhelming significance dawned upon him, that staggered Turkey Doolan. "Right out there?" he said. "With pistols? At twelve mid—"

Turkey was already fumbling for his watch (actually the property of one P. Strom, or thus it was engraved; Turkey had found it atop some loose sheets from a farmer's almanac years before, in a latrine behind a Lubbock restaurant). The watch read only eleven-forty, but Turkey snatched up his boots and shirt nonetheless. "Because I wouldn't take a chance on missing this fer all the free nooky from here to Medicine Hat," he declared. He rushed into the next room.

So there sat the doctor in his nightshirt, calmly drinking something from a steaming mug as if nothing of earthshaking consequence were about to occur at all. "Why, howdy, son," he said pleasantly. "Feeling ballsy after your sleep, are you? Go help yourself to a spot of coffee—"

"Coffee?" Turkey stared at him incredulously. *"Now?* When the notoriousest desperado and the hardest-rock sheriff in the whole untamed West is gonter meet each other face-to-face in a gun shoot? How could any human bean in his right mind sit there drinking coffee at a time like—"

"Now, son," the doctor said, his look inexplicably one of amusement also, "I reckon Dingus Billy Magee is up to some mischief or other right about now, sure as snakes suck eggs.

But you don't rightly expect that either of them two critters is imbecile enough to parade on out there into that pitch-black street and—"

"Huh?" Turkey said. "Well, you heard the feller calling it out, dint you? Why, this is a event folks'll be recollecting about fer jest years, like they does about all Wild Bill's gun battles up to Kansas, or—"

"Wild Bill?" The doctor raised an eyebrow. "Wild Bill Hickok? Now where'd you ever hear about him having a actual—"

"Hear?" Turkey stomped into a boot. "Jest every darned place I ever rode, is all, about how he faced down more foes'n you could count, and—"

"Seems right peculiar to me," the doctor decided, "seeing as how I come from Kansas myself, and the onliest time I ever heard of Wild Bill actually killing even one single person a-tall—I mean not counting in the war or against Injuns, of course—well, it were sure a mite different from what you're talking on. That were up to Abilene in Seventy-one, if'n you're interested, one night when there happened to be some ruckus going on which it were Bill's obligation to investigate, him being town marshal. Now he waits until things is simmered down, nacherly, afore he saunters out, but then jest about the same time, why here comes another feller creeping round likewise, whereupon Bill murders him on sight. Or what I mean, it were sound he murdered him on, because if'n he took time to look first he might of noticed it were his best chum, jest being curious like Bill hisself concerning what the fuss were about. Which is what's likely to happen to you, incidentally, like it done once tonight already, if'n you go poking outside there. But it also oughter make the point somewhat clear that there jest ain't no such occurrence as a pistol fracas where two fellers march straight on up the avenue and—"

Turkey was buttoning his shirt. "Doc, you must of been seeing things. But even if you wasn't, what about say Mister Wyatt Earp then, when him and his brothers and Doc Holliday kilt them other fellers in the famous disagreement over to the O.K. Corral in Tombstone? Now you can't tell me that one dint happen just like—"

"Oh, that were a case where folks jest walked right on up to each other, I reckon," the doctor admitted. "Excepting how it turned out after the smoke blowed away, them misfortunate Clanton riders hadn't had but one lone handgun betwixt the four of them—which the Earps just happened to be informed of in advance, incidentally, since it were Wyatt hisself who'd pointed out the town ordinance against carrying weapons and made them other boys turn 'em in to commence with. So—"

"Aw, well, what's that got to do with anything anyways?" Turkey demanded. "It's still all besides the point to what's gonter happen out there in that street in jest about ten quick minutes, when—"

So now the doctor began to mumble as if for his own conviction only. "Wild Bill were sitting at a poker table with'n his back turned when they shot him in it. Billy Bonney were on his way to carve hisself a slice of eating beef when Pat Garrett kilt him in a dark room without no word of previous notice neither. Bill Longley got strung up by the neck, and Clay Allison fell out'n a mule wagon and broke his'n. That feller Ford snuck up to the ass-end of Jesse James, and John Ringo blowed out his own personal brains, and John Wesley Hardin is doing twenty-five years in the Huntsville Penitentiary." The doctor looked up almost sadly. "But now all of a sudden either Hoke Birdsill or Dingus Billy Magee is gonter become the first individual in modern-day history, outside of maybe in that there traveling show Buffalo Bill Cody done put together to bamboozle a bunch of lard-headed Easterners, who's gonter get kilt by sashaying accommodatingly on up to another feller he knows is carrying a primed firearm in his hand and—"

"Doc, don't tell me no more," Turkey cut in then. "Because none of that applies nohow, since this here's Dingus Billy Magee hisself, and not them others. And you jest don't seem to know it, I reckon, but Dingus is the boldest, fearsomest, most lion-heartedest desperado that ever drawed blood. Why, he's a real modern Robbing Hood, too, who'd loan a pard the actual duds off'n his back. Or you take what he informed me jest the other week, about how he met up with Mister Earp and Doc Holliday theirselves when they was down on their luck over towards the Pecos once, and he dint even bear them no grudge from their previous disagreements neither, as when he'd had to pistol-whip them one time, but out'n pure Christian generosity he give them every red cent he had in his poke. And now tonight—why tonight's gonter be jest the most valiant episode in his whole astounding career, is all."

The doctor considered all that with an expression which eluded Turkey completely, finally returning to his coffee. But Turkey had no more time to discuss the matter anyhow. Because if he himself had waited all these years for something to happen, and then had been under the illusion it had finally come to pass when Hoke Birdsill shot him, Turkey knew now that he had been sorely mistaken. Because that had been prelude merely, had been but the first rude intimation of what lay ahead. "Because *now* is really when it's gonter happen, all right," he told himself, "and if this misbelieving old fud don't know it, well that's jest his poor dumb luck."

So he not only disregarded the doctor entirely but forgot to ask about the vest also, striding rapidly toward the door. "Jest don't come weeping to me when you wanter know the facts of it later," he declared in dismissal.

"Oh, I'll hear 'em somewheres soon enough, I don't doubt," the doctor sighed. "Feller'd almost get the notion it were worth minted money or some such, the way folks is so quick to rush around telling each other about—"

But Turkey had already drawn the door after himself. "Money," he muttered contemptuously. "Don't he know there's jest some experiences in this life you can't never *buy?*"

The street was actually darker than he had anticipated, despite lights that glimmered here and there in houses and saloons, since the moon was lost amid racing shards of clouds. Turkey started to his right, moving furtively and keeping clear of the roadway itself, although peering into its profound, reaching shadows. Unconsciously, he was licking his lips as he went. "Were I *there?*" he enunciated smugly, already practicing, already in preparation for all the long, fecund years ahead, "—why, where else would I of been? You think Dingus would of made a move without he had Turkey Doolan close to hand?"

Deep in the blackness at the corner of a wooden frame house he chose his spot. He was diagonally across from the adobe jail itself, close enough to discern a single hanging lamp beyond a high barred window. Somewhere a coyote howled as if in presentiment, with foreboding and yet expectantly at once, although P. Strom's watch informed him dimly there were perhaps five minutes yet. Turkey decided to slip behind a post on the porch then, an even finer vantage point, since another lamp in a window behind him cast a shallow but precious glow across this immediate section of the street.

Then, abruptly, that lamp moved, terrifying him for a fraction of a second before he realized it had simply been lifted, carried away by someone inside the house. He saw no one, however, glancing rearward too late. So he had just returned to his vigil, shifting to peer into the grim, ominous shadows once again, when the door opened and the woman emerged.

Turkey cried out in genuine concern. "Oh, ma'am, you sure better get back on inside there—"

Startled herself, the woman shuddered as Turkey arose quickly to reassure her. "Begging your pardon for being on your premises," he explained. "But there's about to be this immortal gun duel, you see, involving that famous desperado, Dingus Billy Magee, which I'm sure you've heard of, and—"

Something happened to the woman at mention of the name. In fact for a moment Turkey thought she might drop the lamp. Still alarmed anyway, he snatched it from her, deciding at the same time to extinguish it as a precautionary measure (if pausing for the briefest moment to consider the woman herself first, her face striking him as unengagingly long and marelike, her hair twisted into curl papers for some reason decidedly the worse for wear). "Please now, ma'am," he insisted, "and you'd best hasten, too. Not that Dingus hisself won't shoot straight as a arrow, but that Hoke Birdsill, why he's apt to be fusillading in nine different directions at once out'n sheer terror, afore he finally gets kilt, so—"

"What?" the woman demanded then, seeming to scowl in the darkness. "Sheriff Birdsill will be what? Why, I'm just on my way to the jail myself. What are you—?"

"He's gonter get hisself deceased in this pistol battle with Dingus Billy Magee, yes'm. Smack out in the street here, any instant now, which is why I were suggesting you oughter get youself to—"

"Deceased? Sheriff Birdsill—" She continued to hesitate. "But I'm afraid I still don't understand. Because he and I are scheduled to be—a fight? With actual weapons? In which it is possible that—that Mr. Birdsill might be—might—?"

"Ma'am," Turkey proclaimed gravely, "you can take my solemn true oath on it. That feller Birdsill, he's as good as worm-eaten already. Because when Dingus gets his dander up, well there jest ain't no—"

But then it was too late for explanation. Suddenly— magnificently, gloriously—a revolver shot shattered the night. Turkey Doolan's heart leaped, even as he was instinctively whirling to fling himself behind the post again. "Protect yourself, ma'am!" he cried.

But then just as quickly the exultation, the ecstasy, melted for an instant into panic. Because when he searched the street now, when his eyes strained to penetrate the sprawling, interlaced shadows, he saw nothing at all. Horrified that it might be over even before it seemed to have begun, Turkey could have cursed the woman's interruption, the moment's distraction.

Then a new shot exploded, allowing Turkey to sigh with relief even as he made out the sheriff, Hoke Birdsill himself, in the flash of powder, as he recognized the frock coat which had hovered above him near the livery stable earlier, the derby hat as well. Darkness enveloped the figure again before the sound ceased reverberating, however. Turkey caught his breath, waiting once more.

The next shot came too swiftly, and from too far off, for Turkey to discern anything in its flash. But with this one he did not have to. "Git 'im, Dingus!" he cried. "Git the wick-dipping polecat where it hurts!"

Then he actually did see him after all, saw Dingus, and this time it seemed to Turkey Doolan that not only his breath, not only his heart, but the world itself had stopped for the fleeting, immemorial moment. Because it was the vest that Turkey recognized now, the gaudy red-and-yellow fringed Mexican vest that he himself, he, Millard Fillmore Doolan, had worn that very day and which Dingus had somehow retrieved, which like some charmed protective talisman Dingus had felt indispensable for this ultimate deadly confrontation with his eternal nemesis. Turkey recognized it beyond any doubting as the shadowy, sprinting figure darted through the spillage of light from the doorway of a saloon, as the colors flashed in apotheosis to name the headlong dashing presence of Dingus Billy Magee! Turkey trembled with the thrill, with the consciousness of history itself in the making.

"Oh boy, oh boy, oh boy!" he cried, although oblivious of his own exclamations now, "that dopey old Doc! This'll learn him what a feller kin believe in, I reckon!"

Then Dingus was gone (Turkey had seen him for half a second actually, perhaps less) and silence again flooded the night. There was no visible movement now, Dingus could be anywhere, Hoke Birdsill similarly. So when the next shot came, and no mere revolver's crack this time but the unmistakable boom of a shotgun instead, flashing behind a hooded wagon toward which Turkey was not looking at all, he had no idea who had fired, no way of determining shooter or intended victim. The echo rocked and clattered across the town, a dog yelped in disapprobation—and then the stillness settled again like doom. Turkey's heartbeat ceased one further time. "Dingus?" he whispered. "Aw, come on, git 'im, git 'im!"

Then a sickening, an impossible idea crossed Turkey Doolan's mind, one that he could not have conceived of even a moment before. "Dingus?" he said again. Turkey dared not move.

Yet only the silence persisted, the impenetrable dark, through which an immense sadness stole over Turkey Doolan where he crouched. And then with it, from out of nowhere, from out of memory long years buried now, four lines of poetry came into his head, the only lines of poetry Turkey had ever learned, written by that beloved frontiersman Captain Jack Crawford at the death of Wild Bill himself. Doc was an old turd, Doc's mockery could never detract from their grace, their beauty. As always, they brought tears into Turkey Doolan's eyes:

> *Under the sod at Deadwood Gulch*
> *We have laid Bill's last remains:*
> *No more his manly form will hail*
> *The Red Man on the plains . . .*

And Dingus? If the impossible happened to Dingus, would he too find his bard, would there arise someone to compose the stanzas worthy of this so much nobler life? Turkey felt bereft, a terrible desolation visited him.

But finally now, faintly, at long last he believed he heard footsteps, people approaching distantly. He could not be sure—nor could he bear it any longer. Turkey built himself shaking to his feet.

So he was already feeling his way toward the top step when he became aware of the woman again, when he heard her venture forward through the darkness herself. "What happened?" she whispered hoarsely. "Did it—was it the way you said it would—?"

And then Turkey despised himself for his doubts, for his lapse of faith. Rising to his full height, less in restitution for the affront to Dingus alone than to everything he himself held sacred, Turkey proclaimed, "Ma'am, you could wager your last gold dollar on it. Now a slight portion weren't too distinct, maybe, but it were Hoke Birdsill got his'n, absolutely."

"Sheriff Birdsill, dead?"

The woman's voice was remote, although perhaps somewhat thoughtful also. "Yes'm," Turkey said, peering into the street anew. "Why, I don't doubt, if'n we lighted that there lamp we could be the first lucky folks to view his mutilated remains where they fell. Especially since it don't appear nobody else in town is rushing out awful hasty—"

So he had glanced back once more, waiting to see if she might in fact retrieve the lamp, when a curious sensation of self-consciousness took hold of him. Because the woman seemed to be considering him oddly in the blackness now, looking him up and down intently as if she had not before been truly aware of his presence at all. "Sheriff Birdsill is dead?" she said again.

"Yes'm," Turkey repeated.

And still the woman continued to gaze at him in that odd way. Then her voice changed, however, became almost weary. "You'll have to help me," she said.

"How's that, ma'am?"

"Yes," she said. "Yes. Indeed. Because all this excitement, it's given me—suddenly, yes. This—this chill. In fact it's—"

"Chill?" Turkey said.

"Ch-ch-chill. Yes. Why, I simply may die on the spot. But if you'll take my arm, help me back into—"

"Oh, but ma'am, there's Dingus, and—"

So then he had no choice in the matter, since the woman swooned into his arms. Turkey had to carry her inside.

Thirty minutes later, when he raced to the scene of the fire, he was no more or less immodestly clothed than most of the other townspeople there before him, considering the hour, and even those few who had arrived in relatively substantial attire were already sharing selected garments with the dispossessed prostitutes themselves, a coat here, a shirt there. There was also a prodigality of wholly undraped flesh for Turkey to gape at, in fact, where it bulged and shivered in the fierce light of the blaze. Stark naked, and repudiating any sartorial charity at all, one girl was actually perched screaming atop a hitching rail at the forefront of the crowd, while very near her struggling improbably to disguise a veritable cascade of stomachs with nothing more abundant than a kerchief, an elderly man was shouting hysterically also. Someone identified him as the town mayor. "Our major industry!" he cried. "The foremost attraction of Yerkey's Hole, wiped away in one fell swoop!"

Because it was the bordello, of course, Belle's, blazing like the tinder box it was. The heat was terrific, but no less so than the light itself which flooded the onlookers as, moments before, it had flooded the very bedroom where Turkey had been pacing incredulously, a hand clapped to his skull. *"Defenseless?"* he had been crying. *"Ruined?* Aw now, lady, it weren't *me* dragged us in here tearing off her clothes and mine too like tonight were the first time in your life you ever heard there were such a thing as two folks crawling under the same blankets at the same time fer some other reason than they was both tired, or—*married? MARRIED?"*

He had not even learned the woman's name. He still hadn't for that matter, although the sudden inundation of near-daylight breaking over them had postponed the need to temporarily, had thrown even that calamitous insanity into abeyance. Because even she, the deranged horse-faced creature with the abused curl papers in her colorless hair, had become alarmed then, or curious anyway at the sudden furor in the streets, the commotion. No one had been hurt, evidently, it had started upstairs at the rear, and the main stairway had remained unobstructed for a while. But no one seemed to know its origin either. Flames flickered and hissed among the angular roofs, and within the structure itself the holocaust appeared absolute. "But every stitch!" a whore was wailing. "Every stitch a girl owns!" "Don't fret youself none, honey," a miner reassured her. "You could always come bed down under the sluice with me and the boys."

So he was more distracted than ever when he finally discovered the doctor, still in his own nightshirt and prancing excitedly at the periphery of the crowd. "Lissen," Turkey cried, clutching at the man's flannel sleeve, pulling him even further aside, "what happened? What happened? How did it—?"

"Don't know," the doctor pronounced almost gaily. "But she's a spit-sizzling sweetheart, ain't she? Purtiest durned fire I seen since—"

"Oh thunderation, not that!" Turkey protested. "Who gives a Chinaman's lob about some dumb old fire? I mean before, with Dingus and Hoke Birdsill, when they done what you said they wasn't never gonter do and I said they was, and then they—"

"*Who* said they never?" The doctor turned to eye him indignantly. "Why, I could of told you right from the start, it were gonter be jest as spectacular as—"

"But—"

"Yep. Matter of fact I don't reckon there's ever been one solitary episode in the whole history of human heroism kin compare with it. Why, the way Dingus jest kept on acoming, letting Hoke git in all them first shots, too, and not firing hisself even when Hoke put one bullet clear through the brim of his hat, and then a next one smack across the fringe of his vest, but jest asmiling that there confident, lion-hearted smile until he finally got on up close enough to lift that shotgun where he knew he weren't gonter miss, and then he—"

"He *done—?*"

"Why, sure. And where was you, you didn't see it? Ain't you the eagle-eye weren't gonter miss a trick?"

"Well, I dint. I mean I were right out there, no more'n forty feet away neither, or at least I were until I got somewhat indulged elsewhere. But it sure dint strike me as near light enough to never see nobody *smile,* let alone take notice of no bullet hole in a—"

"Well, I reckon you jest ain't very special in the eyesight category, son. Because I witnessed the whole event clear as well water myself, from down there in front'n my office, and—"

"Your office? But I were ten times closer'n that, and—"

So Turkey was gawking in consternation, even beginning to itch from it symptomatically, when a girl suddenly cut them off with a scream from somewhere beyond his vision. *"Belle! I don't see Belle! Oh, glory be! And it must of commenced up there in her private boudoir likewise. You don't think—"*

"Aw, Belle ain't in there neither. I seed her go tearing off in a surrey, jest a short spell after all that gun fracas took place—"

"Yair, her and one of the girls, whipping them mares like the tax collector hisself were right back of 'em, too—"

"But where—?"

Turkey lost the rest of it in the swell of the crowd, but he could not have been less interested anyway, still dumbly confronting the doctor. "But what come *then?*" he cried finally. "All right, let's jest skip the durned shooting part of it fer now, I mean after. Who got—?"

"Well, that's the only aspect ain't too definite," the doctor admitted. "But the way I calculate it, it looks like they both must of got punctured pretty severe, since—"

"What? *Both?* Dingus got—"

"Well, that's jest theory for the moment, son, because ain't nobody seen ass nor elbow of 'em since. But what they done, they both sort of faded away, into these convenient alleys after the actual disagreement come to a halt, you see. So I don't doubt but where they was headed, they was crawling off somewhere to hunt up separate holes to die in, which a wounded feller'll do, 'times, if'n he comprehends it's hopeless."

"But—" Turkey had to struggle to keep from shouting at the man now, clutching at his nightshirt again. "Now lissen," he sobbed, "jest lissen. How come you don't know no more'n that about it, if'n you claim you saw so durned much of the rest? You ask me, I think you're plumb so full of bullshit your eyes are brown, is what I think, because—"

"Now what reason would I have fer telling fibs?" the doctor asked reasonably. "Of course, ain't neither one of 'em dead in any except the ordinary sense, on the other hand. What I mean, this were their mortal demises, nacherly, but in another way, a brace of gallant, romantic figures like that, especially that Dingus, why he's gonter live on in folks's recollections for just years and years. You might even put it that he belongs to the ages now, like that Henry Wadsworth Longfeller feller, died last year, or General Custer hisself, or—"

Turkey's jaw hung as if ill-hinged. "Doc, lissen, you feel all right?"

"Why not, son? Truth is, it ain't every day in a impoverished old man's career he gets to shed hisself of one unsuccessful line of work and enter into a whole new occupation altogether, I reckon."

"A whole new—"

"Yep. Gonter start me up a Wild West traveling show, sort of like that one of Will Cody's I were mentioning. Because you take yourself now, you're jest a average sort of citizen, wouldn't you claim? And you would of paid, oh, maybe a cash dollar or two to get the true facts of such a historical occasion, wouldn't you? Matter of fact that's how the whole thing come to me, jest after you skedaddled on out'n my office, from when I got to cogitating on how you was so all-fired anxious and all. Now of course it's jest downright fool's luck I happen to be the only living soul's got the gen-u-ine, authentic, eyewitness details, but since it done befell that way I reckon I might as well get me a flat-bottom wagon, and a couple o' actor fellers, and—" The doctor interrupted himself, glancing beyond Turkey. "Why, howdy there, Miss Pfeffer, glad to see you're all recuperated again. You heard tell of all the deathless goings-on, I reckon—"

So Turkey saw her again then too, abruptly forgetting not only the doctor for the moment but even his despair over Dingus himself, itching more violently than ever. She approached quite decorously, however, almost sedate now. "Good evening again yourself, Doctor Fell," she remarked pleasantly. "Yes, a wretched conflagration, isn't it? By the way, I wonder if perchance you've spied the preacher anywhere in the throng?"

"Spied the—" Turkey swallowed dismally. "Oh, now look, ma'am, I already done informed you at least ten times, I ain't but only nineteen years old. And on top of which I—"

So it was a moment before he noticed the gun. It was tiny, a Derringer, but more than adequately persuasive, and he realized too that his own body concealed it from the doctor, or from anyone else. It did not waver, did not falter once as she pressed it cold against his navel where a button was long since missing from his woolens.

"Oh, we was right fond chums fer years," the doctor's voice came obliquely then, from where he had accosted someone else in the crowd. "Real misunderstood lad he were too, sort of a modern nineteenth-century Prince Robin Hood, if'n the facts were knowed. But say, you don't happen to call to mind nobody looking for employment maybe, say some feller round about Hoke Birdsill's heft and build?"

All of which left Turkey Doolan no solace but to further indulge his infested scalp where he stood, wondering in considerably more bewilderment than ever now, just what, after all, had happened, and precisely how, since a good deal unquestionably had, or so it most certainly seemed, while the main roof of Belle's place collapsed in a roar across the street behind them.

"Call me Agnes, why don't you?" the woman suggested.

7

---

*"A brave man reposes in death here.
Why was he not true?"*

Tombstone of Sam Bass, Round Rock, Texas

Meanwhile, back at the bordello, for some time before the fire Hoke Birdsill had been remarkably confused himself. He had not heard the early shotgun blast which indicated that Dingus was escaping from jail, nor did he hear the preacher, Rowbottom, verifying the accomplishment. Once he had been confronted by Belle's protestations of abiding devotion, and her proposal of marriage, sense of the inescapable had clouded Hoke's mind like mist.

So he probably did not realize either, when he finally awoke, that he had fainted. He was still in Belle's bedroom, but he had no notion whatsoever of the time. And why was he undressed, stripped to his woolens? What made his jaw ache is it did?

Hoke could only moan, feeding upon his own malaise. And it was about to get worse, since there remained the rest of it to be remembered now also, the incredible climax of his visit to Miss Pfeffer's, his subsequent meeting with Anna Hot Water in the street. *"Three?"* he asked himself miserably. "Three separate catastrophes all scheduled for the same solitary hour?"

Like some wet, furred beast, Hoke shuddered, burrowing more deeply into Belle's blankets. He lay with his angular knees drawn up against his chest, his eyes closed. "But maybe I'll jest up and die," he speculated hopefully. "Maybe that initial doctor back there in Santa Fe were right that time, and all of them others made a error, and I ain't got but a few months left. A man could face that much, I reckon."

Hoke had ventured only one glance about the room, through a single, heavy-lidded eye, bothered by the lamplight. He had thought himself alone. But gradually now he became aware of sounds behind him, although he did not turn. "Three?" he asked himself again.

But when the sounds increased, almost as if some heavy object of furniture were being disturbed, Hoke at last rolled from the wall. The light remained insupportable, but one of the girls was in fact moving something, dragging an enormous wardrobe trunk toward Belle's rear door, or trying to. She was new to the house, or moderately so, since Hoke scarcely recognized her. "Well, howdy do," she greeted him. "You sure did have yourself a snooze, dint you? Why, you was jest snoring to beat a brass band."

Hoke forced himself to sit, if with inordinate effort, then scrubbed at his mustache with the back of a wrist. "What time's it got to be?" he asked wearily.

"Jest a mite before midnight, I do believe," the girl said.

Hoke gazed blearily at nothing. "You happen to notice my duds around anywheres?"

"Don't seem to," the girl said. Hoke saw now that she was quite young, and fairly appealing also, although somewhat excessively rouged and powdered. Watching him in turn, after a moment she sighed. "Meantimes I jest don't know how I'm *ever* gonter get this trunk down those high stairs now," she told him.

Hoke scowled, considering it without exuberance himself. The trunk was as large as any he had ever seen, and very much like one of Belle's. In fact he was almost certain it was hers.

So then he sobbed. "Don't tell me she's *already* done got readied up for a honeymoon?"

"Who would that be?"

"Jest Belle, I reckon," he said wretchedly. "Excepting what she don't know is that there's two other female personages doubtless preparing to do the same thing at the same—"

"Oh, well, say now, is Belle getting wedded? Truly?" The girl tittered. "And are you the lucky feller? Why, I declare, if'n that ain't jest the wonderfulest thing!"

This time Hoke could only groan.

"Except I wouldn't know anything about Belle's own packing," the girl went on then. "But concerning the trunk, well, Belle said I could borrow that. It's my poor aged mother who's pitiful ill, you see, back home in Texarkana. I jest got the sad news tonight, from a wayfaring stranger who did the kindness of carrying the letter, and I have to hasten to her bedside. I've got a buckboard all prepared down below, too, but I jest can't fathom how I'm gonter get it loaded, I mean all by my helpless self, and—"

"Huh?" Hoke finally roused himself from his stupor. "Oh. Oh, yair." He got to his feet. "You'll pardon my woolies, I reckon. But I'm still durned if'n I kin recollect what happened to my duds."

But for that matter he was unable to remember having undressed either, on top of which his jaw did seem injured now at that. Rubbing it, and troubled by a persistent sense of disjunction, Hoke hestitated briefly. Then, with a shrug, he bent to the trunk.

Hoke blanched. "Whatcha got in there," he asked, "Belle's table silver?" It took virtually all of his strength to jerk it into the doorway.

The girl averted her face with a giggle. "Oh, you know the way a female does collect pretty things, like frilly drawers and such—"

Hoke shook his head. "Well," he breathed. But at least he could see the buckboard hitched and accessible in the yard below. "I'm gonter have to bounce her some, going down."

"Why, I think you're doing right heroically—"

She waltzed down ahead of him while he coped with it as well as possible, which meant assaying no more than a step at a time and having to rest after each. He managed with an extravagant final effort to shoulder it onto the rear rack of the buckboard itself, however, although for an instant it teetered precariously when his knees threatened to give. Hoke staggered against the back wheel, panting.

So he was by no means fully recovered when the pistol shot cracked somewhere in the distance, although it was not merely fatigue which kept the sound from interesting him particularly. Rather it was the girl herself, only that moment mounting the wagon and suddenly, startlingly, presenting Hoke with a spectacular new perspective on her appearance. Viewed from below, massive and pillowlike, her bosom was little short of astounding.

But when a second shot followed, and quickly after that a third, even Hoke found himself disturbed. "Oh, dear me, then they truly are having that dreadful gun battle after all," the girl exclaimed. "Why, it almost makes a lass happy she's leaving, when—"

"Gunfight?" Hoke frowned. "Now who would be—?"

So then a new explosion cut him off, this time the roar of a shotgun instead of a pistol, or so it appeared from the booming echo that slithered and clapped about the town.

Yet Hoke's attention reverted to that improbable bosom once more despite all, drawn there this time by the girl herself as she pressed a hand to it in concern. "But surely you heard the announcement? Heavens, jest about every soul in the house ran on out seeking sheltered locations to watch it from. Because it's that wicked desperado, Dingus Billy Magee, and—"

"Dingus?" Hoke raised his chin skeptically. "Shucks now, must of been somebody pulling your leg, Miss, since Dingus is locked up over to the—"

"Oh, yes," the girl insisted. "Dingus William Magee himself. And the other one is the sheriff of the town, Mr. Broadbill. Mr. Birdsoak? I've never had the opportunity to make the gentleman's acquaintance myself, unfortunately, but I'm certain he's involved also. Yes, positively. Dingus William Magee and Sheriff Birddripping."

"Dingus and—" But Hoke decided there was no point

in attempting to explain, since it was obviously some sort of joke. And the girl was seated now anyway, adjusting the reins. "Well," she said, "I'd sure like to hear how it come out, but my poor aged mother is doubtless sobbing my name even as I dawdle. But I jest don't know what I'd of done without your gallant and manly help, sir."

"Oh, weren't nothing—"

The girl blew him a kiss, bashfully it seemed, then roused her team, and Hoke stood watching with a knowing smile as she moved off. "Now ain't that jest somebody's smart idea of exactly the right girl to play a trick on, too," he mused, "even if'n she sure is built fer better pastimes'n that. Dingus and me. And with the one of us standing right before her very eyes with a slow-rising johnny all the while!"

Yet back in Belle's bedroom, when he still could not seem to locate his clothes, Hoke became perplexed after all. And then when he opened the opposite door, glancing into the main upper corridor, it developed that the girl had been right about that much at least, since the house itself could not have been more quiet. "Belle?" he voiced finally. "Well say, now, jest what in the—?"

So he was wandering thoughtfully back into the room, and exploring the extent of that curious injury to his face again now also, when the puzzlement suddenly became absolute. Because Belle was just arriving then herself, through the same rear door by which he had removed the trunk only moments before. She was carrying a shotgun, or so he noticed tangentially, although this had very little to do with his reaction. Neither did the sight of his clothes at last either, actually, so much as the diverting realization that they could hardly have fit her any better had they been her own. Even the derby rode with a reasonably natural jauntiness atop her tied-back hair.

"Sweetie pot!" Belle flung the shotgun carelessly onto the bed. "And you're awake again. I'm so glad—"

Hoke stopped in his tracks. "And what say to a short snort in celebration?" she went on effusively, not really looking at him as she discarded the derby then also. "Oh, I doubt I murdered the critter, but I scared the crabs right off his smelly bottom for fair, and that's a fact. He sure comprehends Hoke Birdsill is no titty-licker to be trifled with now, by golly!"

"He comprehends what?" Hoke kept on gawking. "Who does? Lissen, Belle, I'd sort of take it favorable if'n you'd inform me jest what all is—"

But Belle had already marched to a cabinet, selecting a whiskey bottle. Beaming from behind it she withdrew the cork with her teeth, then spat that aside. "Yep. Because I waited too durned long since my one previous marriage to let some runny-nozzled twerp of an outlaw turn me into a widow from this present one even before we got around to holding the official ceremony, I reckon. But jest how much of that cotton-picking nonsense did he think a girl would stand for anyways, busting out of jail and farting around challenging folks' fiancées to gunfights, and smack in the middle of my busiest night of the week yet, or—"

"Busting out of—huh? Lissen, lissen, you mean he truly— and she weren't jest—?"

"Oh, but it's over now, ducky nuts." Belle disregarded his confusion. She was pouring two drinks. "On top of which the whole cock-knocking town saw how brave you faced up to him, likewise. I hope your jaw don't pain you too much, meanwhile—didn't give you but a incidental jolt with the side of my fist, was all, especially since you were snoring up a storm from that there swoon you'd had to start with. But here, here, guzzle your booze—"

Hoke was too stupefied not to accept the glass. "Right smart fit in these duds too," Belle continued happily. "I used your Smith and Wesson here, first couple of shots, but then when the mangy little sidewinder actually had the gumption to let fly back at me once, why I jest twiddled that ole scattergun and gave him hallelujah. And he sure lit out pronto after that, I reckon. Well, anyways, drink up, honey jewels, and as soon's I get changed into something a shade more appropriate we'll go fetch Brother Rowbottom. Any of the girls ain't getting reamed can do for witnesses. But here's to it, meanwhile, doll of mine!"

Belle threw down her drink at a gulp, smacking her lips and then wiping them on the sleeve of Hoke's most costly frock coat. Hoke was barely watching, however, still struggling with it. "Escaped?" he repeated. "But I got the durned key right in my pocket here, I mean *there,* but—"

"Aw, sugar boots, now who gives a good gob of spit about how the ballbreaker ever done it? Good riddance, I say, and—"

"But—but there's all that bounty payment, my rewards that I worked so hard to—all of nine thousand and five hun—"

"Now Hoke Birdsill, you don't truly conceive you have to fret your cow-punching ass over any piddling little sum like that? When you're no more than minutes away from being wedded to Belle Nops herself? Why, if I ain't got twenty times that amount in cold cash in my safe here, if not to mention six outsize pisspots full of dust in there that ain't even ever been properly weighed yet likewise, and—"

Belle dismissed his meager concerns with a confident, expansive gesture in the direction of a corner beyond her desk, where the safe had long reposed, although Hoke was still far too vexed to glance that way. Then he could scarcely help himself. Her shriek tore through the roof.

So Hoke himself was barely able to begin to explain then either, since almost before he started she had taken him by the shoulders and was shaking him maniacally, still screaming also. *"Girl!"* she cried. *"Sick mother?* Why there hasn't been a bimbo in this house in ten years who ever knew if her mother was dead or still peddling it, let alone ever got a letter from one or could even read it if she—*in my own wardrobe trunk? And you helped her carry it down? HELPED HER!"*

Hoke was sick. But he understood the remainder of it now, of course, saw it with all the certainty of prophetic revelation. "Oh, no!" he moaned. "No. Because then who was you shooting at out there? Out in that street, at exactly the same time when her and me was standing next to that buckboard and you fired my Smith and Wesson and then the shotgun, who was—"

"Well who in thunderation do you think it was? Dingus Turdface Magee, that's who, and anyway what's that got to do with—"

But Hoke went on with it, torturing them both now, compounding the ordeal. "Sure," he said. "Sure. And meantimes you got a bright frilly red dress somewheres maybe, with a bow jest under the boobies? And a red sunbonnet to match, with strings you kin pull tight so's your hair would be covered up, and—"

"Well blast that too, you've seen me wearing them. They're right in—" Belle whirled, as if to retrieve the garments from her closet. Then she stopped, finally, utterly, for the instant actually rigid with the comprehension. She stared and stared.

"And you never truly seen him neither, did you?" Hoke said. "Yair, because it were dark as a Ethiopian's bunghole out there, weren't it? So if'n I ought of thought to burn the confounded thing six months ago, only I dint, then tonight I should of took it off'n that Turkey Doolan feller and put it into a crate and mailed it to somebody in Siberia. Because it were that vest. All you seen were that red-and-yeller vest and that makes four times now he's done give it to somebody else to get shot at in, only this is the first of the times he hisself went and put on something else in its place. And with a pillow stuffed inside his—"

Belle hit him. Her fist materialized like the hind hoof of a mule and took him on the opposite side of the face this time, slamming him back against the wall and leaving him with his legs stiff but with his heels beginning to slide from under him at once anyway, not trying to stop himself and not really hurt either, not hurting even when he thumped noisily to the floor itself, simply beyond all ability of feeling. "Because I'm probably gonter have heart failure anyways," he thought. "Because I doubtless am."

So it was not until he was climbing into Belle's surrey five minutes later that he began to curse, began to match Belle's incessant, monotonous yet unrepetitive stream word for word with one of his own, reminded faintly of something by the very sound of it also, although he could not think what, nor did he care. And even then it wasn't the money, not the long-despaired eight hundred dollars from his derby hat which had started it all and not the subsequent three thousand from the original rewards either, not that and not this latest, the nine thousand five hundred. Nor was it even the dress which he himself, Hoke, was wearing now, the dress which Belle had only moments before flung into his face while changing hurriedly into one over his pants herself and scattering what remained of his own clothing through the upper rear door and into the yard at the same time, telling him, "Yes, a dress, and the damndest gaudiest silkiest one I own likewise, so maybe the next time you spend half a night being helpful to some other saggy-tooled cluck in one of them you'll have the sense to lift his skirts and see if he's got the right sort of equipment under there or not." It wasn't even that which evoked the oaths.

So it was the pillow, the false bosom. "Because I almost grabbed a quick feel on him," Hoke realized. "I mean her. Him. Standing next to that buckboard and thinking on how all of a sudden I had three durned women to get myself hid from, which it looked like I'd already done give up trying anyways, and I almost grabbed holt of that one right then and there, jest to show myself a man's still got some free choice left. And it wouldn't of been the first time I were in bed with the erection-wasting skunk neither. So now I'm gonter git him. I'm gonter git him now if'n it's the last thing I do on this earth!"

The surrey skidded and slewed, careening out of the alley and into the street, the road. "Yaaaa!" Belle's voice roared and roared, her whip exploding over the mares. "Yaaaa!" Hoke rode with his head held low, fearing the sunbonnet might fail to disguise him adequately even in the darkness, and with a hand clasped across his mustache also, until they had thundered well beyond the town itself along the only obvious trail for the topheavy Dingus to have taken with his prize.

As for the vest, Brother Rowbottom had put that on in all innocence.

He did not understand why it had been left in his shack, although the preacher found it folded far too carefully to suggest inadvertence; in fact it lay atop the very corner of the mattress beneath which he himself had deposited the recently acquired single-action Colt. And the revolver was what he had returned for, of course, after concluding his brief chore. Actually his inquiry had been superfluous; he knew full well that the model would pawn in any saloon for just the figure its previous owner had named.

But then he almost did not go out again after all. Instead, musing absently, he stood for a period as if expecting something, his eyes fast to nothing in particular and yet quite bright, quite alert. What the preacher hoped for was a call, a beckoning, an invocation from elsewhere than in this world. He had been anticipating one for some time now.

Because he had heard such pronouncements before, if not recently. The earliest had come at sixteen, when his family was migrating westward from Tennessee. Indians had attacked their wagon string, killing everyone except Rowbottom himself, although leaving him with his left arm so severely mutilated they obviously believed him dead, and failing to lift his scalp only because, inexplicably, he had already been completely bald for years. Rowbottom wandered in a delirium for days before stumbling into a mining camp where someone was able to complete the necessary amputation.

That was when he first heard the voice, during his convalescence. "Brother, you been chose," was all it said, but he was confident he knew generally what was implied, if not in the particulars. His father had been a sometime preacher before him, as were several uncles. There were perhaps forty miners in the camp, and his exhortations amused them for a time. But when it occurred to him one bright morning to fire the shed in which the communal whiskey was stored, rather than any appreciation of his zeal it was only his height, and his correspondingly exceptional stride, that got him out of the territory alive.

But he was to change his mind about drink as a vice anyway, or have it changed. This happened after he made his way to Oklahoma to live with a relative, one of the preaching uncles. The man accepted Rowbottom as an acolyte of sorts, restricting him to such ministrations as driving tentpegs and hawking Bibles initially, but finally letting him try his hand in the pulpit also. He made no comment afterward, offered no criticism, or not until some weeks later when he suggested that the boy try again. "But this time you might interpolate a bit more hot pee and vinegar amid the words," he said then. This was about three o'clock, with a camp meeting scheduled at five, and he handed the boy a jug. Rowbottom almost fell from the improvised dais half a dozen times. He made twice that many conversions.

So if it wasn't drink, he began to wonder if his special vocation might have to do with women. There was only one in the uncle's home town, or one of the sort he had in mind, and Rowbottom set out with a characteristic vengeance to redeem what he took to be her unwittingly strayed soul. Surprisingly, the whore proved interested in the notion herself, or so it appeared when she cooperated to the extent of letting the boy talk himself hoarse for three consecutive hours, and even supplied him with whiskey of her own when it became evident that this was what primed him. But then when he was barely able to keep his feet she locked the door and proceeded to teach him a thing or two about what he thought he had been talking about. "So I got to marry you," he said, "as a penance. It's the sole way to salvation, fer the both of us."

The woman threw him out then, but he persisted, if limited to remonstrance from beneath her window now. And when even a bucket of slops over the head failed to deter him, she at last seemed to capitulate. "All right," she told him, "since it looks like I either got to be saved from ordinary everyday sinning or else have murder on my conscience to boot. Tomorrow then. You come back tomorrow night and we'll get fixed up."

She had six or eight of her better clients in on it by then, one of whom happened to be the local justice of the peace, the rest ostensibly serving as witnesses. Rowbottom himself failed to discern how any of them were expected to fulfill the latter function in a room where all the lamps had been extinguished, but the woman insisted. "It's more romantic in the dark," she assured him, even squeezing his hand, although the ceremony did not take long anyway. But then when a lamp finally did go on the whore lay doubled up on the floor laughing and the hand he now found himself clutching belonged to a squat, dumpy, incredibly square-headed Indian girl, a Kiowa apparently and obviously as befuddled as Rowbottom himself, if also too drunk to stand.

He was in Sweetwater, Texas, a month after vaulting the whore's window ledge, when he glanced up from a pulpit one evening to find her gazing at him blissfully from the rear of his newest congregation, unpresuming actually, and with the expression on her quadrangular face very much like wonderment at her own temerity, but at the same time waving a small, folded, and already long filthy paper that he understood from the length of the room away would be the certificate, the Oklahoma license. It was only chance that the first horse he spied belonged to a federal marshal. And even then Rowbottom was another full week's ride removed in less than four days, but they had telegraphed ahead.

So he was on the rockpile when the voice came again. This time it said only, "Wait, now," but he might have anticipated that. He had been given ten years.

Two years after he got out he was still waiting. But then when he happened upon Yerkey's Hole, finally, at long last, he began to sense a certain urgency again, a renewed purpose, although he could never fully grasp it. But even the town's name was a hint. "Yerkey's Hole," he asked someone. "You mean it were a famous water well?" "It were a whore," he was told, "name of Yerkey." So when he started to preach at the brothel, it was in the realization that he had best keep his hand in. Because it could not be long now.

Then something horrendous happened to him. He had been in the town perhaps a week and was strolling aimlessly one evening, passing an abandoned sutler's wagon, when she loomed up from the shadows behind it. "You want bim-bam, mister?" she asked him. It was dark, and it had been exactly twelve years. But there was no mistaking that blunt, flat head, that squat form. Rowbottom almost collapsed on the spot.

But a miracle occurred. She was peering directly at him, seeming almost to study him even, yet no recognition crossed her face at all, and when she persisted in hailing him it was only in regard to her original proposition, her modest semiprofessional offering. Rowbottom ran into her several more times in the next weeks, once at last deliberately approaching her wagon in daylight, but by then he was positive she had forgotten. "So that's a sign by itself," he decided. "Because she must of been brung here special, jest for me to understand I'm truly released of that one trivial burden now. Which doubly indicates there's got to be a momentous new Call acomin', and pronto."

So he had been waiting more anxiously than ever tonight, listening with palpable concentration, after he found the vest. And then when he gave up again temporarily, he put on the vest itself only because wearing something, for a man minus one arm, had always struck him as more practical than carrying it. He thought he might sell the garment at the same time he pawned the pistol. That he tucked into his waistband.

So at first, approaching the wagon, he thought it no more than the usual solicitation, although it did strike him as curious that she carried a shotgun.

Then Rowbottom halted, still some distance away beneath a rapidly diminishing moon, remotely curious yet not hearing her too well either, and wondering what had happened to her usual wares, since what she attempted to merchandise now seemed limited to a "mean goose." But something turned him wary also. "You run pretty damn fast," she went on incomprehensibly, and still from quite far off, "for a feller squish out seventeen bim-bam in twenty damn hours, oh yeah. But I think I damn catch you this time, you betcha."

Rowbottom knew a moment of debilitating uncertainty. Could he have misinterpreted the signs somehow? Was this some mysterious new revelation, a delayed recognition after all? He was backing off slowly, not yet completely panicked, when suddenly she sprang.

His stride was still extraordinary. But luck was with him also, since by the time he paused for breath, a good half the town away, not only did it appear that he had lost her but the moon was fully hidden now as well. He waited until he was certain there were no further sounds of pursuit, then ventured on toward the main street. "So maybe His scheme is jest more complicated than I knowed," he was thinking. "Because if'n I got to move on, it were right accommodating of Him to hold off on informing me until I had that money from the pawning almost to hand."

So then she shot at him.

Now this was a development considerably beyond any possibility of immediate analysis, although Rowbottom retained the presence of mind to start running again first, before pondering it. Actually he had not seen her this time at all. But when a second bullet proceeded to gouge a foot-long sliver from the planked sidewalk directly ahead of him, just as he bounded through the spillage of light from a saloon doorway, he stopped long enough to disengage the Colt from his trousers and fire once himself, if only into the affrontive blackness.

Whereupon a blast from the shotgun slammed and clattered about him like the ultimate Wrath. Rowbottom got out of there without further contest then.

He shed himself of the vest as he went now also, realizing that in any light at all it rendered him far too inviting a target. "Anyways I reckon I got the point of it by now," he said. "Not jest git, but git quick." But he held up guardedly in a stand of pines for at least ten minutes before daring even the rear alleys again. Then, making his way stealthily through some cottonwoods behind the bordello, he almost took to his heels one more time, although the furor was only Belle Nops herself evidently, and one of her uglier girls, departing hastily in a surrey.

Then a further and even more portentous aspect of The Scheme was revealed to Brother Rowbottom. For reasons fabulously beyond his own imagining, in the ill-kept yard behind the house someone had discarded a spanking outfit of men's clothing, lacking the trousers but with each remaining item almost miraculously a perfect fit and all of them far more expensively tailored than any he himself had ever possessed. Only the derby hat gave him pause, but not for long. "Because it ain't fer me to go questioning His helpfulness," Rowbottom declared. "And if'n He deems I got to approach that there new calling in style, well that's jest Hoke Birdbugger's poor lookout, I reckon." So he had just stepped into the shaft of lamplight from the open upper doorway, the better to contemplate his transformation, when she hove into view again.

Rowbottom's pulse skipped, even as he commenced to grope hopelessly for the pistol that still reposed among his other clothes some feet away. But Providence had not yet ceased to work its wonders: not only was she no longer carrying the shotgun, but she came plodding toward him so forlornly, and in such abject spirits, that it scarcely seemed credible she had ever pursued him with violent intent at all. In fact when she finally noticed him she reacted to his presence with a gesture almost of resignation. After which she actually shrugged. "Oh, well," she said, "so I don't get Dean Goose, greatest bim-bam there is. So I back to you again, you dud-cartridge son-um-beetch. And I think it damn past midnight now too."

So again Rowbottom had not the vaguest idea what she was talking about, although he was not really listening either, already eyeing favorable directions for flight. And she had begun to stalk him too. But then, backtracking cautiously, he stumbled over the lowest of the bordello's rear steps.

She was at him with a leap.

Rowbottom bolted upward, the least cluttered avenue. The door was wedged open, or perhaps hooked into place, but he had no time to close it anyway. He dove headlong beneath an enormous disheveled bed as she trundled up behind him.

She stopped just short of his derby, where he had lost it ducking under. "All right, you son-um-beetch, where you went?" she demanded immediately. "Because I pretty damn pooped, chase you, chase that Dean Goose feller from jail before, chase him again when I see damn vest in dark out there, damn near get shot too. So I settle for short end now, be wife to Hoke Birdsill. But right damn quick I think, oh yes, hey. So you drag bumpy ass on out or I come scoot down under—which you want, you son-um-beetch?"

So this time he understood just enough—that she had never recognized him after all, that doubtless the whole ordeal had been just that, a trial, a test of his mettle before the final glorious Calling would be proclaimed at last. So he was free to ready himself now, could prepare for the visitation. "Shucks," he said, already sliding back out, "you want the sheriff, I reckon, Hoke Birddiddler. Well, I ain't him, as you kin plainly see. I'm jest acting sheriff fer a brief spell, is all, so he done give me the loan of his duds to make it more official. But if'n you'll pardon me I'll jest mosey on along about the outlaw-catching business then, and—"

"Hey?" The squaw scowled at him uncomprehendingly as he retrieved the derby. Then she went so far as to lift the lamp from its stand, peering at him from beneath it. "Sure ain't Soapy-Tool Birdsill okay," she admitted finally. "But how come is that?"

But Rowbottom was already edging toward the door, unobtrusively, while she peered and peered. Then, glancing that way to avoid any misstep, perhaps he failed to notice it immediately—the slow, speculative narrowing of the eyes, the hesitant pursing of the lips, the profoundly visible evidence of the toils of elemental retrospection. "One-arm feller?" she said. "Ten times I hear people say it, one-arm, bald-headed preacher feller. Couple damn times I see you too, hey. But where I see you before? What your names, hey?"

And then it came, incredulous and exultant at once, with all the apocalyptic resplendence of a trumpet in thunder: "*Rowbottoms! Rowbottoms!* Oh, my husband man, from so damn long I damn near forget whole damn thing!" Maybe she realized she had been holding the lamp, maybe Rowbottom did also. Maybe they both saw it crash into the wall as her arms shot outward, scattering fuel and flame alike, maybe they saw the bed blossom like a pyre. "Oh, my husband man!" she cried. "All these years Anna Hot Water wait, dream of first bim-bam with my husband! Who need that son-um-beetch Hoke Birdsill, who want Dean Goose, when I find my husband lover bim-bam again!"

Rowbottom stood for a time transfixed, mesmerized. Then, when he fled, when he devolved through the door, it was with no thought of the stairs at all, but into space, heedless and unfettered, like a man touched by assurances not of this world—like one who has penetrated The Scheme Itself, who is privy to The Very Word. His feet were already moving, however, even in passage, and he was running when he hit.

It was dawn when Belle and Hoke met the cavalry patrol. By then Belle's rage was insupportable. The moon had reappeared perhaps thirty minutes after they had left the town itself, perhaps twenty after Hoke, chancing to look back, had noticed the fire, and had understood immediately by its very enormity what was burning also, if not how or why. He had said nothing, however, no solitary word, merely casting surreptitious glances across one silk-garbed shoulder now and then as they fled onward, while Belle's own furious intractable glare remained fast to the trail ahead of them as if fixed there hypnotically, and through all the hours since then the road had stretched before them across the mesa like something unspooled. Frequently in the night's fresh settled dust they had obliterated recent hoofmarks with their own, had flung their spume across the stark virginal scars of wildly skidding buckboard wheels. But Dingus himself still raced on somewhere unseen beyond them.

So she was reining in the lathered, foaming team the instant the patrol cantered into view, pausing to sob once out of fatigue or possibly dumb rage again, but then had bounded from the surrey and was rushing to accost the troopers even before Hoke himself fully realized they were no longer moving. There were about a dozen riders, led by a captain whose braid Hoke could distinguish even at a substantial remove. Then as they came on in the lifting gray light he recognized the man, a grimed youth named Fiedler. His entire patrol was haggard and spent. The officer recognized Belle immediately in turn (very few male residents of the territory would fail to) but she allowed him no time for pleasantries. "Dingus Billy Magee!" she shouted even before he had halted. "That slimy, yellow-scrotum'd, dingleberry-picking polecat—in a buckboard, headed this way. Did you pass the—?"

For a moment Captain Fiedler simply gazed at her, his lips puckered. Nor was it just puzzlement, mere astonishment at this disheveled and furious yet familiar apparition so frantically hailing him here in the empty mesa at dawn. It wasn't even the sight of Hoke's striped pants beneath her dress. Because when he began to curse his sudden implosive anger left even Belle's protracted blasphemy wan by comparison. "Because I'll be damned on Judgment Day for a knave," he explained. "Dingus Billy Magee. Surely. Because ever since we ran into the two of them yesterday I've been wondering who he was, where I'd seen him before. Sending us on a wild goose chase after nonexistent Apaches, when there isn't a—"

"What?" Belle cut in, cried in annoyance, "yesterday? No, I'm talking about today, tonight, right on this road, in a—"

"And I'm talking about yesterday, in the afternoon," the captain said. "When we were finally on our way into Yerkey's Hole for a bivouac after a patrol that was already weeks too long and met two riders who told us about a Mescalero abduction raid on a pair of wagons. Wagons that don't exist any more than the Indians do. Pounding our backsides raw over some saddle tramp's idea of a joke, and through it all a bell kept ringing in the back of my mind—where had I seen one of them before? The one who called me Fetterman. Surely. So now I finally remember. It was on a reward poster. The—"

Belle snatched at the man's pantleg where he sat. "Hang it all," she demanded, "now what the fornicating thunder do I give a hoot about that? It's now, tonight, that the mangy little pudding-pounder ran off with my safe and all my life's savings and—on this blasted road I'm standing an this minute, it's got to be this road, in a buckboard with—"

But Hoke's own impatience could withstand no more either. So he forgot why he had not climbed from the surrey to start with, why he had been sitting with a hand shielding his mustache. "In a dress!" he cried. "Don't forget the—"

He caught himself too late, wilting in mortification as the troopers turned toward him to a man in simultaneous amazement. "Why, you hairy-chested old honey," one of them started.

But Belle was already back at it. "Will you *listen,* confound it! Yes, in a dress, him too. And with a trunk, a big wardrobe trunk on the back of the—"

"Dress?" The captain frowned then. "Trunk? Well, surely now, there was a dress. I mean there was a girl, if that's what *you* mean. Why, she passed us not twenty minutes ago. As a matter of fact I thought she might be in distress at first, but she told us she was just rushing off to get married. But I don't understand what—"

But Belle had already spun back to the surrey. Half boarded, she paused anew. "One hundred dollars for each man!" she shouted. "Or hell's bells, never mind that—there's that nine thousand or more in rewards for the first one puts a bullet up his giggy. But on top of that I'll—"

She did not have to pursue it. Only Captain Fiedler hesitated briefly. Then he too had whirled his mount and was pounding after the others.

Nor could the surrey keep up, of course. So half an hour

later they were still steaming across the broad vast mesa itself, in full daylight now and some moments after the troopers themselves had disappeared far ahead where the road twisted northward into an abrupt high upthrust of stone hills, into a defile, when they heard the shooting, the rifles. "Git 'im!" Belle shrieked instantly in approval, harrying the thundering mares even more hysterically, "—git him good now! Fill the miserable meat-beater so full o' lead even the vultures'll vomit when they chomp on him!"

"But—" Hoke swallowed in disappointment, reading the same probability into the sounds and certain then that his own meager claim to the rewards was being irrevocably superseded (not by any means accustomed to the idea of a marriage that would render them inconsequential yet, either). But then he became moderately perplexed as well. "Because lissen," he yelled, or tried to over the horses, "how long kin they keep plinking at him in there anyways? How much of a fight kin he—?"

Because the firing still went on. As a matter of fact it cracked and volleyed so incessantly that if he hadn't known better Hoke would have estimated a good many more than ten or a dozen rifles to be involved. "My gawd," he commiserated then, "they truly must be massacrating the misfortunate critter at that, the way they're—"

"And I say more power to 'em!" Belle dismissed him. "Pulverize the twerp!" she screamed enthusiastically into the wind. "String him up by his prunes and take target practice! Pop so many holes in the varmint he'll leak until hell sprouts flowers!"

Except it wasn't Dingus.

It took only an instant, less than that, as the surrey finally careened into the gorge itself amid high sheer walls, as it screeched precariously around the first unnavigable turn and into sight of the troopers at the same time, for Hoke to understand it had to be something different, something more. But then he was too busy to look, snatching at the reins where Belle had suddenly abandoned control in favor of the brake now but missing them completely as the amok vehicle pitched and lurched and twice almost overturned completely, stopping only after it had slewed about in a full circle to wedge itself against stone. Hoke was already leaping from it before that, however, as the bullets whined and ricocheted about his fluttering skirts, diving for shelter behind boulders where the troopers themselves were pinned down by the relentless fusillade from somewhere beyond. He buried his nose into the shiny blue serge of the soldier across whose sprawled backside he had landed, too startled to be shocked or terrified yet, although hardly failing to hear Belle's own instantaneous new outburst despite all. "Indians?" she roared at Captain Fiedler. "*Indians?* Now great bleeding eardrums, it was you yourself jest said there ain't a hos-tile Indian within six counties of this place, so how could—"

"Well, you'll pardon me if I don't exactly call these peace-able," the officer yelled back, scarcely in need of the irony as a new hail of bullets whistled and chinked overhead. "But at least they've most likely done us the favor of dispatching your outlaw friend for you, since he couldn't have been more than fifteen or twenty minutes ahead of us coming through the—"

"But my trunk!" Belle wailed. "My safe! Where's—"

And then the shooting stopped, abruptly but absolutely. Hoke himself had not previously moved, save to dissociate himself from the trooper's bottom. But when the silence persisted he finally raised his head, finding the others near him beginning to better deploy themselves also, behind what appeared a fairly secure natural barricade, a fortuitously banked upheaval of jagged split shale. "And now what?" Belle was demanding. "What are they—?"

"Just regrouping, I'd imagine," Captain Fiedler specu-lated. "Or maybe debating an attack, since it's pretty much a stalemate the way we're situated at the moment." Hoke could see the youthful officer kneeling, eyeing the terrain. Then the man turned to his sergeant, indicating something behind Hoke himself with a gesture, speaking more quietly.

Hoke saw it also, however, comprehending. Close at hand,

yet probably obscured from the vision of the Indians themselves, a narrow crevice broke upward through the shelving
toward higher ground. And almost immediately the sergeant
darted toward it, obviously for purposes of reconnoitering.

"I've got a hunch we can outflank them," the captain
elaborated. "It might work if we're not too badly out-
numbered, which we don't seem to be. Let's hold fire and
wait, now—"

So they sat. Nor did the Indians renew their own fire
either, except for those moments during which random
troopers showed themselves fleetingly, evidently satisfied
merely to hold the patrol at bay. Then for some moments
only Belle's irrecusable mutterings alone punctuated the
calm:

"That lamb-ramming, rump-rooting, scut-befouling,
fist-wiving, gopher-mounting, finger-thrusting, maiden-
head-barging, bird's-nest-ransacking, shift-beshitting, two-
at-a-time-tupping lecherous little pox. On top of which he
wasn't born either, he was just pissed up against a wall and
hatched in the sun. I'll—"

But the sergeant finally reappeared, though it struck Hoke
at once that something boded ill. In fact the man made his
way toward them so thoughtfully, and in such evident distraction, that he almost exposed himself more than once.
And then when he reached the captain for a long moment
he merely stared, not saying a word.

"Well, drat it all, did you see them, man? What's the—"
And still the sergeant seemed wholly disconcerted, although
at last he nodded. "I saw them. Yessir. Right clear in fact.
But—"

"And? So? Can we take them? Can we get—"

"We could take them easy. Yessir. But the thing is, we
can't. I mean we can't fight. Because—"

"Can't fight? Says what? There aren't that many of them,
are there? And if there's a good tactical approach from—"

"It ain't that," the sergeant said, although still he seemed
incapable of coping with whatever it might be instead. "I
mean we don't even need tactics. But that's the whole point.

I mean, it'd be almost too easy, because it ain't Injuns. I mean, I reckon they're Injuns all right, but—"

"Listen now, listen!" Captain Fiedler struggled to check his anger. "Sergeant, are you sick? Will you for heaven's sake tell me what's—"

"It's squaws."

"It's—*what?*"

"Squaws. Ain't one single buck warrior down there; not a one. You kin hang me for a chicken-stealer if'n every single Winchester ain't being shot by a female. And—"

"But—but—ambushing a patrol of United States Cavalry? *Squaws?*"

The sergeant shrugged. "Well, it don't *sound* no more loco than it *looked,* I reckon. But it's even more loco'n that. Because there's some men down there too, all right, maybe ten or a dozen of 'em, but they ain't fighters—jest the old limp-dicked kind you see on reservations, maybe. And there's a decent-size remuda likewise, like the whole outfit's migrating somewheres, or was, until say no more'n ten or fifteen minutes ago. But now there's this one tepee sort of half throwed up against a couple of trees—more like a improvised lean-to is what you'd call it—and there's this buckboard setting near it. With that there wardrobe trunk still on it, yes'm. But what I mean, all the old men are doing, they're loafing around like somebody told 'em they had to wait on something for a spell, while over by the lean-to—well, there was this one squaw, real purty young wench too, jest getting herself all stripped down bare-titted and crawling inside. So it's only the other sixteen who's deployed out behind them boulders keeping a bead on us, and—"

"It's only—" Hoke cut the man off without intending to, the exclamation voicing itself. And then he was almost afraid to pursue it. "Sixteen?" he asked hesitantly. "You mean counting the one in the lean-to, nacherly. You don't mean the sum total of them squaws is—"

"Jest what I said. Sixteen and one, which if'n you know how to add better'n you know how to git dressed, comes out to—"

But Hoke had already stopped listening. He had closed his eyes also. "Seventeen?" he moaned. "Seventeen?" Finally he faced it again, not able not to. "But jest tell me slow," he said. "Down amongst the old men, you dint maybe notice one of them chewing on a nice appetizing boiled wood rat, sort of fer nourishment betwixt meals? Or if'n he ain't hungry at the moment, then doubtless he's still wearing a expensive derby hat anyways, and—"

"Well, yair, come to think on it I did see one with a derby, but what is—"

"Nothing," Hoke said. "Nothing at all." His eyes were shut again, and his head was lowered. "Excepting it'll be at least twenty hours now, or anyways that's what it took him the last time when they was camped up to Fronteras, and I don't reckon there's gonter be none of them let us cut it no shorter neither, not until they all durned sure git their bellybuttons squished out, so—"

But he was not being understood, evidently. Or perhaps he had mumbled even more than he realized, slumped against a rock and not even caring, not for the moment. *Dean Goose?* he heard Belle shouting at him. And then she was shaking him once more too. "Because he's the greatest *what? Who?* Now what the blazes kind of word is—"

But this time he didn't answer at all, already banging his head against the boulder behind him where he sat, quite hard, although quite deliberately also, in that profoundly impotent, ponderous rhythm of absolute and unmitigable frustration, of futility beyond hope. They had to restrain him physically.

And he was right, because it was to be the twenty hours indeed, give or take an apparent meal or two, and by then Captain Fiedler and his troopers would be long departed for Yerkey's Hole. But there would be another problem then too. Because it had been approximately six o'clock in the morning when it commenced, and at dusk, at twilight, it was only the twelfth squaw who was emerging from the tepee, the thirteenth who was entering. So they knew it would be under cover of darkness that it would cease. "Or when the damned thing just falls off him altogether," Belle said.

So when the next morning came and the Indians were furtively gone at that, and the buckboard at the same time, without there having been a single sound for Belle or Hoke to hear, without a trace now either, there was only one boon, one saving grace. There still remained only the one direction for him to have taken with his burden. At the crack of dawn, and with the further benison of well-rested horses, they were storming after him again.

"And I'm even almost glad," Belle said. "I almost am. Because this time I'm gonter have less mercy than a aggravated rattlesnake. I ain't even gonter kill him now, not right off. I'm jest gonter bury the little pee-drinker up to his neck Apache-style and prop his mouth open with a stick and let the ants do it. As a matter of fact I'll sell tickets."

Hoke said nothing. He hadn't for most of the day and night of the waiting. Now he simply rocked in place, not even jouncing with the sway of the surrey either, but almost as if in some esoteric, mystical periodicity of his own, like a creature irretrievably lost to meditation. He still wore the dress, the bonnet, but he had stopped thinking about both. He clutched his Smith and Wesson in his right hand, its hammer uncocked but with his finger welded against the trigger for so long that he had lost all feeling there without knowing it.

They were perhaps four hours into daylight when they met the wagon, a dilapidated old Conestoga, creaking in desultory indolence toward them behind equally aged, unperturbable mules. There were two women aboard, neither of them young but not old either, wholly anonymous, undifferentiated in their drabness as well. Hoke did not even avert his face now, did not hide his mustache as Belle questioned them. "Why, yes," one of them acknowledged, "no more than an hour ago. Indeed, a lovely girl. We chatted briefly. Her husband recently passed away, and she's returning home to Wounded Knee."

Then Hoke awoke to something after all, remembered it, dissuading Belle with a gesture even as she was about to urge the horses onward again. "Yair," he said. "Because it's a day and a half already, and I'm about to start on the harness." He restrained the two drab women in the covered wagon. "I ain't particular," he said. "Hardtack or jerky or—"

They gave him biscuits and cheese, willingly enough, if still dubious about his costume. And then Hoke refused to eat while riding too. "Because it ain't good fer what ails me," he said, "not after what he done put my intestines through already. But anyways, time don't matter no more. Sooner or later, that's all that matters. Today or next week or someyear when Mister Chester Arthur ain't even President no longer. Because I got a whole lifetime I'm gonter be contented to devote to it now."

So he was standing at the side of the Conestoga, dipping water from a lashed-down canister, when he overheard the conversation. The women had paused to rest now themselves, although their dialogue meant nothing to him:

"Oh, dear, sometimes I'm afraid we just won't find him after all—"

"And it's our own fault too, for waiting so long to look. Six wasted years, when we should never have let him leave to begin with. Never—"

"Yet it frightens me at times, the extent of our obsession. Why, even that young girl these people are following, would you believe that even she reminded me of him slightly?"

"Oh, but by now he must be far too manly to resemble any young lady—"

"Of course, it was only illusion. But I've longed for him so deeply, so deeply—"

"I too, I too!"

"Well, shall we move on, Miss Youngblood?"

"Let's, Miss Grimshaw."

Hoke strolled back to the surrey.

Three hours later it happened. Afterward, Hoke would find it difficult to remember how, since he was never aware of the exact point at which logic ceased and the other, the intuitive, took hold.

Because he had been squinting ahead at the abandoned farmhouse for some time before it did. They were going fast also, passing only the first of the once-cultivated fields in fact, and there were no signs at all, nothing to indicate that Dingus had even taken this same road, let alone might have stopped. Yet suddenly Hoke knew, felt it even before realizing that he felt anything at all, because his left hand had already lifted involuntarily to obstruct Belle's right, staying the whip. "Hang it," she demanded, "now what the—?"

And then it must have been in his face too, the same certainty, although he still could not have explained, nor did he even glance toward her. But somehow there was contagion in it, in his posture alone perhaps, because Belle slowed the team at once. The house itself was roughly a hundred yards off the road, the gutted barn beyond that, and they were only now abreast of both. "What?" she whispered. "Do you see—?"

They went another thirty or forty yards before they stopped completely, and after that several moments elapsed in which neither of them moved, in which only the horses snorted and heaved in their traces. Belle was clutching her shotgun. A single jay swooped by in the heat, in the hot bright calm afternoon glare.

Then Hoke was running. And this too, this without question now was instinct, some queer spontaneous impulse beyond thought, because still he had not seen him yet at all—had bolted from the surrey and was sprinting across the eroded ancient plowditches and had actually covered one third of the distance to the house before he did, before Dingus appeared. Dingus still wore the red dress, although without the bonnet now, without the pillow as well. He had emerged leisurely, carrying a shovel, strolling toward the barn.

And then perhaps Hoke was thinking again at last, had begun to think, to remember, the lost money, rewards gained and stolen and re-established and lost again, frustration that seeped to the deepest marrow of his bones, the aggregate affront to his soul itself. Perhaps he was, because he told himself, "Yair, but he's kilt now, at last he's kilt and I kin get some peace." But there remained something scarcely rational about him at the same time, even then, since he did not shoot but merely continued to run, if not quite without reason then recklessly at the very least since the furrowed earth had begun to give beneath his boots now, was crumbling with every stride so that he slipped and flailed and almost fell more than once. But he was lucky too. Dingus himself had still failed to notice him, still strolled there casually.

Then Hoke saw Dingus see him. And still he ran, heedless, the Smith and Wesson cocked in his fist now but with that still not raised for use yet either, toward where the other had abruptly whirled, where Dingus himself now stood likewise without firing or possibly even unarmed since he made no move to withdraw a weapon from his garments, from the red frills. Probably it was incredulity more than surprise which held him, momentary incapacity at the sight of Hoke in a dress of his own and with the irrationality patent in his very headlong attitude itself, as he stumbled and tripped yet came on maniacally like some infuriated hellbent mad scarecrow and still not firing but worse, looking as if he did not intend to fire at all but instead would obliterate Dingus through the sheer lunatic inertia of the rush alone. Hoke plunged on as if to run right over him.

Dingus threw the shovel. He was at last turning to flee then, however, so that Hoke did not have to swerve or even falter as the ponderous spinning missile shot wildly past his ear. Dingus darted back toward the house, his skirts sailing. Hoke was less than a dozen strides behind him.

He had closed half of that gap when Dingus disappeared as if swallowed by the earth itself.

Hoke pitched onto his face. In less than the duration of a blink against the sun, against the flung dirt from his heels, miraculously, Dingus was gone, Hoke was absolutely alone in the field.

But Hoke was truly thinking again now after all. Or perhaps not, perhaps this too was intuition, since it came so quickly that even bafflement was precluded for more than the first fleeting instant and after that he was up and plunging onward as before. "Because it's jest a well," he told himself and it was, although the mortared stones that had once encircled it had crumbled away and lay now scattered some distance beyond the pit itself. It was not wide, not four feet across. It was not deep either, clogged with earth and debris. From perhaps eight feet down Dingus was gaping wide-eyed, truly astonished—and at his own predicament rather than at the sight of Hoke now—but with his hands already braced against the shaft at his either side and posed as if to defy gravity and human capability and his own bewilderment at once, as if set to sprint back up and out again. "Now Hoke," he said. "Now Hoke—"

Perhaps Hoke heard Belle also then, the single prohibitive outcry from somewhere behind him as she hastened across the field herself. Hoke was panting, and his chest filled and fell, but he did not wait. He did not even listen.

Steadying the Smith and Wesson in both hands, aiming with infinite deliberation, Hoke emptied all charged chambers into the narrow well.

The shots banged and echoed in the shaft, reverberating out across the low hills, repeating fitfully. Hoke Birdsill filled his lungs hungrily with the sweet warm air, with the pure cleansing taste of exoneration at last, of release. He did not look; there could scarcely be less need. With his shoulders squared as if for the first time in decades, unabashed by even the dress now, he strode back to meet Belle.

She had stopped some yards away. Nor did she move now, facing him with a kind of grim, constrained ferocity as he approached. Finally, wearily, she sobbed once. "Find it," she said.

"What's that, Belle?"

"What we came after, you banana-head. The safe. My money. You can use that shovel he ought to have brained you with. It shouldn't take you more than eight or ten months to dig up every square foot of ground out here that he might have picked to—"

"But—"

She got around to hitting him then, a response he was growing accustomed to. He went down stifflegged, precisely as he had the last time, save with no wall to slump against. It didn't hurt. He sat forlornly for a moment or two, just watching while she herself gazed stolidly about, wishing remotely that he were back in Yerkey's Hole with young Fiedler and his womenless troopers. The captain seemed intelligent, the last sort to be engulfed in such sexual maelstroms. Hoke wished advice.

"All right," Belle was saying at last, "maybe we'll have some luck. Maybe we'll find fresh dirt, if the ratholing little exhibitionist didn't have time to disguise it proper."

"I were digging up graves and making them look ordinary again when I weren't but eight years old," the voice informed them then, distantly, muffled and hollow yet hideously, sickeningly familiar. "You kin poke around from now 'til Dooms-day and you ain't gonter find it, not unless I get drugged up out'n here first."

Slack-jawed, Hoke had sprung to his hands and knees. This time when she hit him it was only out of relief.

"Get a ladder," she told him disgustedly. "There must be one in the barn. If you can find the barn."

"And git me some new boots," the voice contributed. "You mule-sniffing blind cockroach, you done put a leak in the toe of one of 'em—"

It was a cemetery in actual fact, roughly a quarter of a mile beyond the barn itself, where four rotted wood crosses marked the remains of the family whose farm it was, or had been. And he was right. The grave he had contrived for the trunk was identical with the others, undiscernible as new.

Belle stood above him with the shotgun while he performed the excavation, although Hoke had to help with the lifting. "But I weren't never very exceptional at physical doings," Dingus said. When they finished hoisting it aboard the surrey he turned to grin at them affably.

"Sort of a shame you caught up so quick," he decided, "since it would of nacherly been a even pleasanter joke if'n I dint return it fer a week or so, like I planned. Oh well, it were enjoyable anyways. But seeing as how it's terminated, I'll jest mosey on along then, I reckon—"

"Say your prayers," Belle told him.

"Aw now, Belle, you're smiling when you say that, I reckon—"

"I'll give you three minutes, twerp."

"But—"

Dingus studied her dubiously, then looked to Hoke instead, although Hoke had hardly anything more comforting to offer. In fact he had begun to nibble his mustache in anticipation, all the promise renewed again despite its brief debacle. He was even eyeing the shotgun greedily.

Belle merely gazed at him askance.

"Aw, shucks now," Hoke pleaded, "them durned forty-fours jest weren't never worth much fer accuracy to start with. But if'n I had a chance with that there scattershooter— especially it still being me he done give the heartache to fer the longest spell. On top of which I could get them rewards again, and—"

"We'll both do it," Belle decided abruptly. "Why, sure. A gentleman and a lady planning to get spliced, they ought to start sharing their satisfactions early anyways—"

"Married?" Dingus popped back into the conversation eagerly. "Well, say now, let me be the first to—"

"You'd put a curse on it," Belle said. "And that's a minute gone now. You better get to praying, I reckon."

"Oh, I weren't never the praying sort," Dingus went on undeterred. "Jest sort of a old Emersonian, were all. But lookie here, I ain't truly a bad nipper at heart. Matter of fact I doubtless wouldn't of never wound up the way I done, if'n I'd had a mother to guide me in this life. And jest to show you there's no hard feelings—why, here, I'd be obliged if'n I could give you a wedding present. It's—"

The shotgun lifted threateningly as Dingus fumbled in his skirts, but it was only a watch. "Don't keep time too hot," he admitted, "sort of antique. But it's all engraved right smartly too. Here, what it says, it's *'To my darling Ding, he rings the bell.'* It were my—"

"*What?*"

Belle snatched the object from his hand. Then, inexplicably, staring at it, she turned livid. "Why, you immoral, dirty-livered skunk, where'd you get this? You even went and stole this somewheres too, didn't you? Well, hang it all, that's the end now, the absolute mother-loving end. Because if—"

"Huh?" Dingus backed off more in perplexity than protest as she glared at him. "Now confound it, Belle, I never done stole it neither. Like I jest started to remark, that watch belong to—"

"Lissen, you lying-mouthed little pussy-poacher, I gave this identical timepiece to somebody exactly twenty years ago, before the ornery polecat went and lost me to a white slaver in a faro game and started me on the road to ruin. Here, where it says he rings the bell, it was supposed to say *Belle,* with an *e,* but the jeweler made a mistake. From me to him, my first husband. And *Ding* was short for—"

"*Dilinghaus? You?* You done give that watch to—"

"What? Dilinghaus, sure. Of course. But how the thunderation would you know that, you conniving little—"

"But that were my daddy's name. That were—"

"Your da— But then—but then you're—*not the beautiful baby son they made me leave behind?* Not the baby I've wept for in my secret misery for all these long, long years—"

"And then you're my—my—"

"*My baby! Oh, my precious, precious baby!*"

"*Mommy! Oh, my very own, my long-lost mommy!*"

Belle threw aside the shotgun. Dingus discarded the Colt he had been surreptitiously manipulating from beneath his skirts. Hoke stood amazed with the wonder of it, but already beginning to sob for a sentimental old fool himself, as they rushed to each other, as they embraced.

It was well after midnight before he was able to slip from the farmhouse. Stealthily he led one of the horses to the road.

There were no saddles, so he was still busily improvising a workable bit and reins when Dingus approached with another of the animals. For a time they gazed at each other without expression.

"All right," Hoke said finally, "I'll say it quick. And it ain't even the idea of getting hitched, which maybe I done been a bachelor long enough to accept anyways. And doubtless I could even get used to you being a part of it. But not when she made me kiss your boyish brow goodnight like a daddy oughter, which is jest one step more'n any self-respecting man could take. So meantimes what's your reason?"

"All that talking she done about the three of us turning respectable," Dingus said. "About going somewheres that nobody knows us and living like good Christian folk. Because I been there before, with every danged relative I ever got tied to. I'll take my chances on remaining a orphan, if'n it's all the same."

"How far will she chase us, do you reckon?"

Just south of San Francisco, an ill-guarded freight office supplied the price of their fares. She emptied several lethal devices from the wharf about seven minutes after the gang-plank was raised, but the damage to the smokestack was nominal. They had to share a cabin with two other gentlemen, having been unexpected, and while they got on with both, it was the youth, Doolan, for whom they felt the larger affection. Rowbottom's flatulence drove them above decks often. Otherwise poker for modest stakes occupied them until Valparaiso.

The Ballad of Dingus Magee

It was dusk that night when he rode on in
To the town of Yerkey's Hole—
He was only a boy just turned nineteen,
Yet the gallows was his goal.

For Dingus Magee was a desperate lad,
The worst New Mex. then saw—
'Twas plain he'd come with aroused intent
To trample on the law.

But the law in town was a sheriff bold,
Hoke Birdsill was his name,
And Hoke himself was no man's fool
In that deadly shooting game.

So both were calm, and hard as rock,
Though bullets flew like hail,
As they staged their mortal duel that night,
In the street before the jail.

And then what occurred was an awesome thing
That cowards fear to tell—
For some say Hoke took so much lead
He sank clear down to hell.

But others remark 'twas queerer still
For Dingus Magee, alas—
They claim he crawled off limp to die
While caressing a maiden's knee.

Yet none can name, and name for true
The place where each was laid,
And none can judge, are heroes born,
Or are they only made?

But sometimes still, in Yerkey's Hole,
Where Belle's Place used to lie,
It seems you can hear the banging yet—
"That's them!" old-timers cry.

Refrain
But sometimes still, in Yerkey's Hole,
& Cetera.

Mrs. Agnes Pfeffer Fiedler
Yerkey's Hole, 1885